Southern Exposure

Travel can be one of the most rewarding forms of introspection.
Lawrence Durrell

Also by Helen Pereira:

Magpie in the Tower	1990
The Home We Leave Behind	1992
Wild Cotton	1994
Birds of Paradise	1997

All published by Killick Press

Southern Exposure

Helen Pereira

The Key Publishing House Inc.

Copyright © 2007 by Helen Pereira

Editor: Frances Rooney
frooney2002@yahoo.com

First Edition 2007
The Key Publishing House Inc.
Toronto, Canada
Website: www.thekeypublish.com
E-mail: info@thekeypublish.com

ISBN 978-0-9782526-2-5 paperback

Cover Design and Typeset Olga Lagounova
Cover Photographs © Lori Bristow

Library and Archives Canada Cataloguing in Publication
Pereira, Helen
    Southern exposure / Helen Pereira.
ISBN 978-0-9782526-2-5
    1. Canadians--Foreign countries--Fiction. I. Title.
PS8581.E648S69 2007   C813'.54   C2007-904833-1

Printed and bound by MCRL in China. This book is printed on paper suitable for recycling and made from fully sustained forest sources.

The Key Publishing House Inc.

These stories were written with love for my grandkids, from A to Z: Alec, Anna, Jeremy, Lori, Nigel, and Zak

Acknowledgments

The author wishes to thank Frances Rooney, Bette Hall, Linda Hutsell-Manning, and Janine Elias Joukema for their support and editorial comments during the writing of this book. She is especially grateful to the David and Julia White Colony in Costa Rica whose generous, pleasant staff bear no resemblance to those of the Snake Ranch.

Different versions of some stories appeared in earlier publications by Killick Press and in literary journals in Canada, USA, and Argentina.

Contents

Brazil: Green and Gold

Mission to Recife

Road to the Sky

A Bouquet of Roses

Green and Gold

Mission to Recife

When Annie steps onto the bus she realizes that she has let the missionaries do it to her again. The bloody hypocrites have conned her into going to the black market to do their dirty work for them.

The black market is not new to Annie. Before leaving for Brazil, she and Carlos had been briefed at a tea in the administrator's home about how and where to change American dollars for *cruzeiros*. Annie had worried about what to wear to that important tea. After several changes she had settled on her good suit. The suit she always wore when she needed confidence. She had also worn her sister's pearl necklace, an amulet reserved for those occasions when she wanted to make a good impression. She had promised herself that she would not talk too much, knowing that she always did that when nervous.

Annie had thought that the project administrator, Cecil Mowat, and his wife, Edna, were too eager to put the *tecnicos* at ease. Cecil's eagerness had made her nervous. So had his record of foreign postings of which he and his wife spoke casually. "Remember that time in Bangladesh, darling? Or was it India? No, Tanzania."

That afternoon, Edna Mowat, dressed in a dazzling purple sari, had asked Annie, "How do you take your tea?"

"With milk, please."

At her response, glances were exchanged.

"But *how*, my dear? Milk first, or after?"

"Whatever. Does it matter?"

"Of course it matters!"

Then Barbara, Edna's friend visiting from England, had giggled. Annie stared at her. From the maroon and gold of Barbara's silk pantsuit, Annie guessed that she had been posted to some place sort of Buddhist. Tibet? Bhutan?

After Barbara and Edna had exchanged glances, Barbara smiled at Annie and knelt before the tea tray to announce, "Let me pour you a *proper* cup of tea, my dear." She poured milk in first and explained that this was "the correct way." Then she rose and brought Annie tea and a plate of buttered scones.

Yes, Annie decided, balancing tea and scones on her knee, Barbara had for sure been somewhere Buddhist. I wish that we were going to a country like that, where they wear really exotic clothes. I'll have to lose weight before I can fit into a Brazilian bikini. Brazil would be easy. Brazilians drink coffee. I can do coffee.

When Cecil began his orientation spiel, Annie expected advice about handling servants, getting immunizations and where to learn Portuguese. Practical stuff.

Cecil had begun, "Buy yourselves sturdy money belts for bringing U.S. dollars into Brazil and for trips to the black market in Recife." He had smiled at the *tecnicos'* surprised looks. "Not to worry," he continued, "It's all very open down there."

Upset, Annie tried to catch Carlos's eye but his gaze was riveted on Cecil, who added, "You'll get the best rates at The Galicia, a little hotel behind the beach in Recife."

Annie had squirmed. Black market? Smuggling money through Customs? Never! She had been about to interrupt when Carlos shot her a warning glance.

Doug, another *tecnico* going to Brazil, asked, "What about Customs? What if they search us?"

Cecil smiled. "They won't. See these?" He held up a cluster of little red books and gave one each to Doug and his wife Tanya, and to Carlos and Annie. "Present this with your passport. No questions will be asked and you'll get to the head of the queue. And business class seats if they have them." After these advantages had been pointed out, lawbreaking sounded sweeter to Annie. She managed to get through tea and scones with a minimum of crumbs and pearl-twiddling, but had been relieved when they thanked and bid good-bye to Cecil, Edna and "Babs"— as Barbara had insisted she be called.

The next day when Carlos sent Annie out to buy money belts, she had refused. "I've never broken the law. Never! I just won't do it." Carlos had persevered, explaining that black markets helped the poor by bringing capital into the country.

Though his arguments never convinced her, she was tired from packing and relented. She had gone to Sears and had slunk around, searching for the counter that sold money belts. When she found it, the clerk brought out a selection to choose from. Leather, cotton; thin, thick. She chose sturdy linen ones in two sizes. His and hers. Bonnie and Clyde.

Cecil's lecture and her Sears trip had not only changed her value system — it helped her to make a decision. She had withdrawn two thousand dollars U.S. from her bank account. You never know, she had thought. Some day, I just might want to take off. I can tell Carlos it's for shopping.

Shortly before leaving, she had learned that Doug and Tanya were not only bringing extra dollars, but watches and calculators to sell on something they had airily referred to as the "grey market."

"We might as well get all we can out of it," Tanya had explained to her. "Everybody else does." Tanya, Doug and their two teenage sons were declaring calculators "for personal use," but to be sold to wealthy Brazilians. Gift-wrapped watches were presents for nonexistent relatives in Rio.

Annie kept this information to herself because she knew that Carlos would go for it, but mostly because Tanya's "everybody else does" had evoked her mother's warnings. "You don't jump off a bridge just because everybody else does."

Going through Customs, Annie felt edgy. She also noticed a certain thrill. International intrigue. She handed the inspector her passport and her little red book. After he returned them with a smile and said, "Take it easy," Annie's guilt had resurfaced.

After settling into an apartment in Lagoa Grande, they had needed Brazilian currency for groceries and salary for Fatima, their *empregada*. Carlos had told Annie it would be best if she changed the money. "It wouldn't do for the locals to get a bad impression of me." Out of concern for Fatima, Annie had complied.

She had accepted The Galicia clerk's low offer to discourage Carlos from making her a mule. Furious, he declared, "From now on I'll handle these matters."

The bus to Recife swerves around a corner. Annie looks at other passengers. All shabbily dressed and poorlooking. In Brazil, the poor travel by bus. Because Annie doesn't drive, it's how she travels. Another of her habits that causes Canadians to gossip. Carlos disapproves of her Recife bus junkets but she finds excuses to go there and escape from other Canadians and the missionaries.

She enjoys traveling alone. Being alone.

Weekends, Carlos drives them to the little hotel where he changes U.S. dollars at premium rates. *Tecnicos* also go to Recife to get drunk and escape. When Annie goes alone, she heads for the airport, buys a beer, reads English magazines and savors her day. Then, late in the afternoon, she returns to Lagoa Grande. These escapes have kept her sane. So far.

Canadians soon dispensed with wearing money belts in Brazil's heat. Older, foreign-posted types had advised, "You only need those things going through Customs."

The missionaries knew all about the Canadian practice of changing money at the black market. Of course, Annie thought, they consider themselves to be above this, so they've conned this Canadian into carrying a check from a Texas bank for five thousand dollars to change on the black market. Just like Carlos, they explained that it would not do for them to set a bad example to parishioners and insisted that the money she changed would do more good if it raked in more *cruzeiros*.

Annie looks out the window and sees arching palms form a curtain over the road. To reassure herself, she pats the big handbag that carries a paperback, her wallet, passport and an ID that refers to her as *Dependente do Carlos Da Costa*. The handbag also contains the little red book with a maple leaf on it that permits Canadian *tecnicos* and their spouses to breeze through Customs. She smiles now, as she remembers how shocked been when she first got the red book.

On a seat across the aisle, a mother nurses her baby under her shawl. Why is she taking her baby to Recife? To escape an abusive husband? To attend a funeral? What about that man sitting up ahead? Does he work in Recife? Is he leaving his wife behind? Is he going to another woman?

Annie wonders whether to treat herself to an airport visit. Carrying so much money, she should really hurry home and hand it over to the missionaries. *Damn.*

Mid-way, the bus swings into a stop where passengers get off for rest and refreshments. Against Brazilian custom for a woman alone, Annie orders a beer and carries it to a table, turning away from men hanging out and drinking *cachaca.* The man who had been sitting ahead of her also orders a beer. The mother carries her baby to the washroom. Annie downs her beer. After the mother and child leave, she heads to the toilet. It's a dreaded stop on this trip. Flies and cockroaches climb over wads of tissue piled in the corner. She grimaces, pees, then washes her hands and walks outside to enjoy the sun, the clean air. Now the mother leans against the bus, holding her baby. The guy from in front appears, followed by the driver and some new passengers. Annie returns to her seat; the mother and baby to theirs, the guy up ahead to his. She pats her handbag, then reassured, she dozes.

Noises from the street; taxi honks, trams. She wakes up and looks out. They are near the bus depot, within walking distance of Gringo Palace, which is what Canadians call The Galicia, "the little hotel behind the big ones at the beach." Here Annie will change the missionaries' check while the owner, *Senhor* Medeiros, pours her beer or cognac.

He likes Canadians because they don't bargain for better rates. He sees himself as their friend, gives them drinks and remembers their names.

Annie follows the mother and child from the bus. The guy in front leaps off. She confirms departure times with the driver and strides over to Gringo Palace.

She walks through the heavily palmed path and into the resort. Macaws jeer from hibiscus trees, a monkey leaps from a branch and scampers toward the hotel as if warning of her arrival. She passes mango trees where oversized fruit hangs from branches.

The worst is over. She is always glad to be here because she really loves this place.

A woman at the front desk looks up at her.

Annie says, "*Bom dia. Onde esta Senhor Medeiros? E preciso de falar consigo.*" When the clerk smiles, Annie, unsure of the language, thinks she has made a mistake. The woman rings a bell and gestures her to sit down. The same drill as when she comes with Carlos.

Waiting, she looks across the verandah at clusters of mango trees. Medeiros is proud of these mangoes and gives them to Canadians.

"*Ah, bom dia Dona Annie! Tudo bem?*"

"*Bom dia, Senhor* Medeiros. *Sim, tudo bem.*" Annie smiles and waits for him to switch to English.

"You have come alone? Your husband did not accompany you?"

"He had to work."

Medeiros shrugs. "You are brave. Come, we will visit in my office."

The secretary smirks. Because Annie is breaking another taboo by meeting a man alone? Or because she knows it's a charade, that Annie is here on business?

Senhor Medeiros holds the door, points to a chair beside a table, takes down a bottle of cognac and glasses from a shelf behind him. He pours, gives a glass to Annie, clinks it against his and asks, "How may I help you?"

"The usual. A check to cash. A big one." She opens her handbag, takes out the check and passes it to him.

He inspects it. "American?"

"Yes."

"Ah yes, the Holy Ones. Are they your friends?"

"Not really. They help me shop at the market."

Annie worries. What if he won't cash the check?

He nods, writes a rate on a piece of paper and shows it to her. The amount is higher than last week's. She wonders whether Medeiros likes her or if the rate went up. She says, "Okay. That's good."

Medeiros rises. "Wait a minute, please."

He leaves and returns with a small metal box, places the check beside it, opens the box, counts out money. It makes a huge heap; they both notice this and smile. Now comes the hard part. Medeiros says, "Please, you must count."

Sweating from heat and anxiety, Annie regrets ever getting into this. She is hopeless with numbers and poor with money. This is a large amount of money, a huge responsibility.

"Take your time, *Dona* Annie," he says, topping her cognac.

She sips, counts; recounts; nods acceptance.

Medeiros reaches across the table and wraps elastic bands around the wads of *cruzeiros*. He puts them into a bag and gives it to her.

While Annie stuffs the bag into her purse, Medeiros watches, concerned.

"*Dona* Annie, have you had lunch? Please, join me before returning. You shouldn't travel alone with such a burden when hungry."

"Lunch sounds great. Thanks."

He leaves and returns with a waitress carrying a tray, dishes and cutlery. She sets platters of chicken, shrimp and salad on the table.

Medeiros says, "Please, help yourself."

The trip and anxiety have made her hungry; the cognac has loosened her tongue. Annie eats heartily, answers questions. She tells him about her family in Canada, about snow, about skiing and hockey. He smiles, prods for more.

Finally, she downs a tiny cup of dark coffee and exclaims, "That's the best meal I've eaten in Brazil."

When she asks for her bill, Medeiros will not let her pay. "It was my pleasure, *Dona* Annie, to have your company." He not only walks her to the door but drives her to the bus depot. "Please come again, *Dona* Annie," he says. "Any time."

"Of course." She offers him her hand. The alcohol, food, his sympathy and interest, have made her happy. All by herself she has made a Brazilian friend. A man who never even tried to make the usual passes, a man who just seems to like her. She decides that she will visit him. Often. She will confide in him, will tell him about herself and all her difficulties.

When returning, she relaxes on the bus and plans her account of the day's events. One version for Carlos and another for the missionaries. This time there's a different crowd on board, but Annie is not preoccupied by them. At the halfway stop she gets off and stays outside, smiles to herself in the sun while gloating over her adventure. She returns to the bus and dozes until traffic sounds signal entry into Lagoa Grande. At the depot, she gets off and looks for Carlos.

He is leaning against their car, talking to Marcus, his lab assistant. The two men are animated, laughing. When he sees her, he turns away from Marcus.

Annie is sure that Carlos has told Marcus about her trip. It's the sort of thing he jokes about. His crazy wife.

He helps her off and says, "How did you make out?"

"Great."

"You did a dangerous thing," Marcus says. "You should never travel alone, men will take advantage."

"Nothing happened."

Disheartened by her lack of interest, Marcus leaves.

Carlos asks, "What rate did you get?"

"The same as last time. Medeiros was boring as usual."

"Olive and Martha asked about you. They'll come tonight to pick up their *cruzeiros*."

"No problem."

"Do you want a pizza? Fatima went home."

"Okay."

They stop for pizza and beer. Annie downs her beer, toys with the pizza.

At home, Carlos goes into the study. Annie undresses and showers. As she dries off, the phone rings. She wraps herself in the towel and picks up the phone.

Olive says, "We've been so worried! We said special prayers for you. Last night at prayer meeting, we didn't explain it to the congregation, but asked them to pray for a Canadian on a mission for our church. We're so happy! Now we can buy little chairs for the Sunday school and an organ. All because of you!"

Annie tells them about her trip and about the man up in front on the bus, who "seemed to be following" her. Olive passes this information on to her husband, the preacher.

"It's a good thing we prayed," her husband tells her. "That man sounds dangerous."

"We'll be right over," Olive says.

"Okay," Annie says, and hangs up. After changing, she gets her handbag and takes out the paper sack containing *cruzeiros*. As she counts it, she thinks, I could cheat them and they'd never even know. They expect the rate quoted last week.

She fingers the bills and looks at the bookcase.

Inside *The Ugly American*, on the second shelf from the bottom, she has hidden running-away money. American dollars for a flight home in case life gets unbearable. Or for a flight somewhere exotic in case she ever gets bored.

She returns the *cruzeiros* to the bag and waits for the missionaries.

The Road to the Sky

In his sleep, Carlos flings his arm across Annie's shoulders, his heavy leg across her hip. She wants to get up, but wonders, get up and do what?

Oh . . . Something nice. Birthday. No. Old. When my kids phone, I'll feel better.

She tiptoes into the tiled bathroom to shower and lets hot water soothe her aching shoulders, then turns on the cold to enjoy the tingle along her spine. She towels herself dry, slips into her housecoat, returns to the bedroom. After slathering her face and arms with sunscreen, she looks at Carlos deep in sleep, his arm across her pillow.

She envies how easily Carlos gets lost in sleep. At first, she liked waking up and leaning on her elbow to admire him. His long lashes and sloped cheekbones. Not anymore. Each day she finds less to admire.

He eats enormous helpings of Brazilian food and has acquired jowls and a paunch. Although tall, he does not carry weight well. When Annie suggested, "Why don't you cut down on rice?" he retorted, "What's wrong with you? I look better now. Successful."

He likes his new weight. She has caught him admiring himself in the mirror; stroking his moustache and smiling.

She goes to the wardrobe to dress but decides to stay in her housecoat. Why make an effort just for him?

Her family and friends had warned her. "You're too old to change, too different culturally from him. Besides, why has he been a bachelor so long?" She had wondered about that herself. A bachelor until he was forty-two? He explained to Annie that he had not married because, as the oldest son in a large family, he had responsibilities. If he felt responsible for his family, she wondered, why did he speak so badly of them? She should have listened. Shouldn't have let him whisk her off to Brazil just because at the time it had seemed like a solution for her exhaustion.

In the kitchen, Fatima rattles dishes, cuts fruit. Annie savors the smell of Brazilian coffee and hurries to the dining room.

She eats breakfast alone because she never knows how the morning will go and doesn't want to ruin the day with quarrels. Morning is her favorite time, breakfast her favorite meal, so she has chosen to eat it alone.

She enjoys Brazilian breakfasts — papaya, pineapple, mangoes; strong coffee with steaming milk.

Fatima greets her. "*Bom dia, Dona Annie. Tudo bem?*"

"*Sim,*" she lies. "*Vou bem, obrigado.*"

Annie's eyes fill. She misses her kids, friends, country, snow. The kids will call today for sure, she thinks. It's my birthday.

Setting the table and watching her, Fatima asks again, "*Tudo bem, Dona Annie?*"

"*Sim, Fatima, vou bem.*" But everything is not all right. Annie has decided to skip her Portuguese class. This will infuriate Carlos. His temper scares her. He had shown anger in Toronto, but not like he does here. Is it the stress of a new job, she wonders, or does he feel more in control now that I'm his wife? Living in his culture? Does the heat make him edgy? No, he's always been edgy but was never around long enough for me to find out what sets him off. When neighbors hear him yell at me,

I'm embarrassed, but glad that they know what's going on.

His shouting is not consistent with his need to impress; the image he presents of being a good guy, the easygoing guy.

The first time she cooked rice on Fatima's day off, he had stormed from the kitchen, dumped the plate in the garbage and eaten at a restaurant. Blaming herself, she sought advice from the wife of an East Indian professor who taught her to let rice sit and plump in its steam. Now, when Annie cooks rice, it is perfect. Fluffy, each grain separate. When Carlos continued to complain, she knew his dissatisfaction came from his own rage or from something about her he couldn't stand. She did not apologize, would say, "Great. Those people on the street will appreciate your food," calmly forking mouthfuls while she seethes with rage. In a battle of self-control, she'd win. But a physical contest? Ah yes, the neighbors.

Carlos showers, humming loudly. When he's angry, he hums. It's a signal to watch herself or she'll be a target. Then she is prudent, on her best behavior. She remembers in Canada, how controlled he had been. "So gentle, for a big man," her neighbor said. He'd charmed the neighbor because he is a charmer. Carlos charms waitresses, clerks, strangers who don't know his history of being fired for losing his temper. At one company he'd struck his boss; at another, decked his supervisor. He told Annie he was a victim of prejudice because he was an immigrant and seen as a threat because he was more brilliant than his superiors. She had actually bought his version.

Immaculate, he strides to the table and sits down. Fatima brings him hot milk and coffee.

He is surprised to see Annie in her housecoat. "Aren't you getting ready for university?"

"I'm not going."

She has been studying Portuguese each morning; afternoons and evenings struggles through the newspaper, dictionary in hand, and now can even tackle crossword puzzles. In another attempt to fit in, she learned to embroider like a proper Brazilian lady. For a while these concessions worked. Carlos agreed to let her swim alone at the club; to go out for a run.

"I'm skipping class today." Annie says, pushing out her chair. It squeaks on the tile. She carries her coffee to the window and looks outside at the sun rising up red behind the Barbarema Mountains. On the street in front of their apartment, she sees a beggar forage through garbage cans: purposeful and business like as he searches, sorts and selects bread to eat, tins and bottles to sell.

As Paulo, the janitor, slouches out, his two little kids surge after him. The beggar heaves the bag over his skinny shoulder and moves on. Paulo tends to plants around the building and turns the water on. His kids are about two and three, Annie guesses. She smiles as she watches them dance barefoot, their little brown backs swaying and swinging. This sense of rhythm here charms her. Even babies move as if dancing before they walk; jiggle tiny feet, swing in their mothers' arms. When the kids scramble under the sprinkler and squeal as water sprays their shoulders, they remind her of Andy and Margaret when they used to play under the sprinkler.

Carlos pulls out his chair. Silence. Annie turns to see Fatima clear the table. Carlos stands with his hands on the back of his chair, waiting.

He wants to ask me something, Annie thinks. She waits. Carlos walks to the door, refusing to look at her.

I'm making things worse, she decides, so calls, "Carlos? It's my birthday. I'm staying home. The kids will telephone. I'd hate to miss them."

He returns to kiss her on the cheek. Dammit, she thinks. Is that the best he can do on my bloody birthday? A Trappist monk could do better. She knows now that what she once thought was shyness is disinterest. Or disappointment.

After the door closes, she goes to the study to finish a letter to her daughter. When she rereads it, she sees that it is filled with spelling errors. Her brain, freed from English, is confused, without boundaries. It must be that. She is frightened; needs to grab her past, hold it.

She has not been to the museum for months but decides to go there today to break the wait for a call from Canada. She needs to have time alone, just thinking and enjoying. Besides, it is very beautiful there. All the cool statues, all the brilliant big flowers.

She crosses the street and passes a man carrying a tiny white coffin on his shoulder. She shivers and hurries into the museum courtyard to sit on her favorite bench.

Now her skin is brown, her hair sun bleached. She feels that she belongs under the poinsettia.

She reaches for memories. The kids will phone tonight; will call me mother. Martha will call me Nana. I will speak English. I will know who I am.

I am Annie MacDonald da Silva. I was born in Kettle Valley, British Columbia, Canada. I am forty-eight today.

Will Martha remember me? Will Andy have a new girlfriend?

I can't remember Margaret's voice. People say she sounds like me.

At home we had Black Forest cake on our birthdays.

When we played "Happy Birthday" on my music box, I always cried.

She had given the music box to Margaret because leaving for Brazil seemed final and she wanted precious possessions left with the right people. Tim's paintings to Phoebe; family snapshots to Andy, mementos to Margaret, who hugged her and cried, "I was afraid you'd give the music box to Andy." Annie's brother Pete had given her that music box on her sixteenth birthday.

"Birthdays are important in Brazil and are occasions for lavish celebrations. Especially the first, because of the high infant mortality rate." She had read that in the *Foreign Experts' Orientation Handbook*.

At least my kids grew up.

She remembers the man with the coffin. Gooseflesh forms on her skin.

It's so scary here, so scary. For weeks after arriving, she awoke disoriented. Heat, the man in her bed, a strange room. She'd changed her name, country, language, status. And seasons. The reversal of seasons confused her.

She had trudged over snowbanks in Toronto, fighting wind in her parka and snow boots when she went to pick up a new passport in a new name. The next day she was whisked into summer heat: shed heavy clothes in Rio and arrived in Recife sweating in a cotton dress. Pale faces of welcoming Canadians at the airport stood out among the dark *Nordestinos*. When she complained of the heat, they told her to enjoy it, warned of a rainy season ahead; of daily drenching and deadly isolation.

It had been too much for her. Every day after Carlos left for the university she went to the museum, herself a stony white figure seated on a bench in the sculpture courtyard; felt white, white, under orange bougainvillea, purple jacaranda. Red poinsettia trees splashed color from their branches, dropped bloody petals on grey tile.

I'm in *Lagoa Grande, Paraiba, Brazil*. My name is Annie MacDonald da Silva. I was born in Kettle Valley, British Columbia, Canada. Yes.

Dazed, she squints behind her sunglasses, grasps the bench with desperate hands. In Toronto there were roles. Mother, social worker. Here, there are no roles, only Carlos to prompt her. The more she remembers her past, the more unreal it becomes. In Canada, they spoke English and she was fluent, in control. In Brazil, she became aware that she had squandered English like a spendthrift. Here, they speak Portuguese and at first she resisted the language as one resists accumulating currency in a country one passes through. She groped through the messy purse of her mind for words, only to find the wrong coin. It was harder when she became proficient, worst of all when she dreamt in Portuguese. Dreams are her soul's territory. When she complained to Flavio, her language instructor, he distressed her even more when he replied, "Wonderful! That happens when one finally accepts a new language. It's a kind of surrender."

Before, she had lived alone, come and gone as she pleased. Now she is accountable to a husband and he to her. War escalates; border clashes occur when either nears the other's territory. Despite Flavio's explanation, she still owns English. Carlos claims Portuguese.

In Canada, Carlos had seemed exotic. She was charmed by that, although she knew he felt alienated and courted her because he needed approval. She was Canadian born and he was an immigrant. There, because she had advantages, he deferred to her opinions and tried to please her.

Now, in Brazil, he feels at home. Although he towers above the slight *Nordestinos*, he is dark, he belongs. He has become flamboyant, Latin; his gestures open.

There are new rules for her here and Carlos enforces them. At first, he would not let her swim alone at the club. In company, he answered questions put to her and expressed what he decided were her opinions. By the time she translated a contradiction, the topic would have changed. Here, he has the advantage.

A whole hibiscus bloom flutters down from a tree and alights near her feet. A tiny pink parasol. She picks it up. Tropical flowers overwhelm her. Their wild colors, their sensual shapes. At first, they complemented her new life with Carlos. Sensual and mysterious. The tropics. Brazil.

The flowers she remembers from childhood were different. Tiny yellow buttercups grew in fields beyond her father's garden; mauve rooster-heads hid among them. In spring she hiked to the slough with friends to search for violets. The slough was magic; wet, dark and cool. Their shoes made sucking sounds in the mud. They would call out in triumph when one of them found a patch of velvety purple violets. Deep, deep purple with orange-striped throats. Rarely, someone might find a ladyslipper. Yellow or purple, a speckled wild baby orchid. A treasure carefully carried home and admired.

They sneaked through the slough to the railroad line and put nails on the tracks for the roaring train wheels to flatten into little knives. Had taken turns running across the track when an engine chugged up. Annie was skinny, not athletic like her friends, but when they competed to see who was the bravest, who would wait the longest before darting in front of an oncoming engine, she won.

She shakes her head, remembers. She'd searched for the exotic, had taken risks, even then.

She'd balked at leaving Canada. Carlos spent weekends at her house, drove her to the rec center to swim. After, he picked up a pizza and a bottle of red. He'd been a diversion. She was amused by the way he intrigued her colleagues. Most of them unmarried, in and out of relationships, these counselors. New partners were praised during the courtship, diagnosed after the break up as immature and controlling. Annie wonders about that. How come we diagnosed clients in the first interview, but not our own partners until after months of intimacy?

Carlos had surprised her, one Friday. "We're having dinner at a Greek place on the Danforth. I want to talk to you." Pleased at the departure from the swim-and-pizza routine, she leaned back in his car. "Great! Let's go to the Odyssey. They have the best lamb. And roast potatoes. I'm starving."

When he ordered a bottle of red wine and insisted that it be from Chile or Argentina, Annie protested. "I won't drink anything from those countries. Besides, here, they expect us to order Greek."

He smiled. "There's a special reason. We're celebrating." After the waiter poured their wine and left, Carlos raised his glass. "To our new life."

"What new life?"

"Our life in Brazil. I've accepted a two-year contract there. We'll have to get married. There are provisions for families. I discussed it during my interview. We're in!"

"You're in. I'm not going. I like my work and I'm not

leaving Andy and Margaret."

"It's time they led their own lives. They don't need you."

He was hurt and angry because Annie had not appreciated his great surprise. He'd thought she would be thrilled. He drove her home, packed his belongings and left.

She'd been relieved. He was too intense. His intensity was exciting, but it tired her and she was already over-tired. After their breakup she realized this. She began to enjoy her old friends again and spent weekends sprawled out in her garden reading.

When she became ill with mono, her doctor ordered rest. Home alone, the days dragged. She cried. Depression went along with mono, friends said. They telephoned, but avoided her. When Carlos dropped by to pick up his guitar, he was attentive and persuasive. "You're rundown, burned out. You need rest, sun. A change. This is fate."

He moved back and cared for her, tempting her with tropical fruit. Pineapples, papayas, mangoes.

"You could have this all the time," he said. "And a maid."

At the time, it sounded wonderful. Sunshine, swimming, no work. They were married at city hall a week before they left. Margaret threw a champagne wedding reception and farewell party for them.

Annie fingers the dead hibiscus. She is tired of leisure, depleted by the warmth she longed for in Canada. Brazil is not the answer. Carlos is not the answer.

The sun moves up, shining down through huge red petals. It's noon. Lunchtime. She slouches across the street toward the apartment. The click of her sandals echoes as she climbs the marble stairs.

Carlos waits, talking to Fatima. Annie joins in, asking

about his work. He rambles on about the lab, his technician, Marcus, and the man's conquests. She has caught Carlos off guard, asking him about subjects he knows she finds boring.

Today they could have a really big fight. Should she risk it?

She watches him eat two huge servings of chicken and rice. She has stopped asking for potatoes. Potatoes, he has told her, are for gringos.

Carlos sleeps after lunch, like a Brazilian. Annie swims or reads. When they first arrived, she read English books. They fought over those books before leaving Canada. They were allowed to bring five hundred pounds of household goods; her crates of books were half this amount. Carlos protested and unpacked them. She packed them again. Again, he unpacked them. The night before their freight was picked up, he packed them.

How she had needed those books in early weeks! Reading English kept her from panic, like touching bottom in strange water. Although now she can read Portuguese, today she sets aside Amado in favor of Graham Greene. Hell, she thinks. It's my birthday. I'll do what I bloody well please.

Her rereading of books infuriates Carlos. An engineer committed to the electronic age, he sees books as obsolete and her habit of rereading them bizarre. For Annie, every time she rereads a novel it is different because she is different.

She hears him move about in their room. As he stops at the study door on his way out, she holds up a book for him to see. To see that she has returned to English.

Her ploy is so obvious that he ignores it.

He says, "Francisco and Marcia are throwing a *churrasco* tonight. It should be fun."

"You go. I don't want to miss my call."

"I thought you liked Marcia. And you love barbecues!"

It's Francisco I like, she thinks. He writes poetry and sends me Brazilian literary quarterlies.

"You never told me anything about tonight. I'm waiting for my call."

"Well, think up a good excuse if Marcia phones. I told Francisco we'd go."

She snaps. "I resent you making social arrangements! Why didn't Marcia call me?"

"It's the custom here."

"For God's sake, don't mention my birthday. You know what a big deal it is with Brazilians."

He stalks out.

The afternoon drags. Annie wants to swim, but reluctant to leave the phone, picks up embroidery. She is working on a tablecloth. A great discovery, embroidery. Simple and repetitive. Embroidery lets her fantasize but gives her something to show for it. No one knows she is really thinking.

Carlos knows. It drives him crazy if she embroiders when he's trying to start a fight. Her retreat into no man's land, a new maneuver, leaves him stranded with anger. She is a small woman, proud of an ability to manipulate this six-footer.

Fatima comes to the door and leads her into the dining room. She points to a doily on the table. She has made it for Annie's birthday. She tells Annie that she is a saint, that she loves her like the Holy Mother.

Annie touches the doily, exclaims, "*Cual coisa linda!*" and wonders, what will I ever do with that? She embraces Fatima before she leaves for the day.

Annie is brooding over embroidery when Carlos returns.

He pours rum and tonic, hands her a glass, raises his.

"Happy birthday."

She barely touches her drink. She moistens silk orange floss between her lips and threads the needle. She squints as she holds the needle up to the light. She is thinking about the man with the coffin, about information she read in the foreign experts' handbook.

Carlos blurts, "If we go to Marcia's we'll have steaks. It'll do you good to get out."

"When?"

"Oh, around eight or nine o' clock. You know Brazilians. Why don't you phone home and get it over with? It'll be my present."

"No."

At nine o'clock she puts on the new red blouse and long skirt he brought her from Rio. "Let's go. They could at least have phoned. I'll be damned if I'll call them on my own birthday."

It's not birthdays they celebrate here, she decides. It's survival.

Dressed up, she feels happier as she slides into the car. Carlos watches, approves.

As he drives past her favorite funeral parlor a body is being wheeled in. It is her favorite because she likes the name, *O Caminho ao Céu*. The road to the sky. There are many funeral parlors here because so many people die. In this heat bodies are wheeled in and buried the same day. Coffins line the sidewalk for prospective buyers. There are several tiny white ones, like the one she saw this morning.

Funeral parlors here are as stark and grim as Annie believes funeral parlors should be. In Canada she rushed past funeral "homes" as if they were unlucky. There, she hated them. Plants, phony solemnity. Reception rooms, unctuous attendants. "Funeral homes"? Who lives in them? In Northeast Brazil, death is death. Funeral parlors, open to the street, look like shabby little service stations. Stores selling the hardware of death. Body preparation and mourning take place at home, except for families rich enough for church burials. As if compensating for the grimness of their wares, these stores are given elaborate names. Annie delights in translating them. "The House of Our Blessed Virgin Mother," "The Palace of Our Lord." She found "The Road to the Sky" to be the most imaginative. She is up on funeral lore because in the event of her own death or Carlos's, their contract provides for their bodies to be returned to Canada.

The man wheeling the body inside disappears.

"Have a good flight," Annie cracks. Carlos hums. It's his warning hum. She tries again. "I hope Marcia has her animals locked up. The last time we were there I thought I'd go crazy. Her making a pizza with that damned parrot flying around. It shit on the cheese. That monkey of hers should be sent back to the jungle where it belongs, the poor thing."

He doesn't respond, though usually quick to defend Brazilians. Annie admires his restraint. He's getting pretty good at games, too, she thinks. Without embroidery.

They join their friends on the patio of Marcia's back-yard. Some guests are dancing, their bodies swaying in the shadows under heavy green trees. Others are eating steaks and washing them down with Brazilian beer. Annie loves Brazilian beer, but tonight chooses wine. Francisco and Marcia have good French wines. Besides, it is her birthday. She looks at the steaks and wine and thinks, Yes, this is my secret party. I'll have fun. It really is beautiful here.

She remembers childhood birthday parties in Kettle Valley. Such strict formats. Two kinds of fancy sandwiches, jelly and whipped cream for dessert. Homemade birthday cakes. Games before and after lunch. Pin the tail on the donkey; musical chairs. Always the same presents. Handkerchiefs, ankle socks, rayon panties. Practical.

Imagine, remembering that.

At least these people here don't know it's my birthday. She looks around, glad that she wore the red blouse and skirt, glad that she exercises and watches her weight. The other women wear bright colors, long skirts; flaunt their sleek arms and shoulders. They are all bare, brown, beautiful and young. Annie knows that they've been visited by their manicurists because their fingers flash bright, red-tipped nails. She hates them all.

The men wear open-necked shirts. When Francisco slips out of his sandals and walks barefoot on the patio, Annie watches him. He's slight, wiry. Her eyes linger on his feet. They are beautiful. Small, high-arched. Carlos wears socks in his big sandals. Annie knows that though she fears big men, she sees them as being protective. She feels something electric, sexy, about slight men.

Francisco, like all Brazilian men, is aware of his effect on women. He sees Annie staring at his feet and sits beside her. She moves away. He moves closer. She wonders what to make of this in Brazil. The pressure of his shoulder could mean anything. Touch is so easy, so ambiguous here, that it's hard to interpret.

She appreciates the Brazilian need for physical closeness. On buses, strangers cuddle close; on streets, nudge in passing. Most Canadians hate this, but not Annie. It reminds her of her family. The physical affection, touching. Good-night hugs and kisses. Kisses when leaving or returning, no matter how they felt.

There is loud laughter. Marcia's monkey, Evva, is the center of attention. Evva is tiny, about the size of Annie's forearm, and has the run of the yard from a long chain. She's a lonely monkey, away from her jungle, Marcia tells them. She says that Evva has fallen in love with a cat. They cuddle at night and snarl at each other by day. Evva, as if sensing she is being discussed, performs for guests by doing gymnastics in an avocado tree — swinging, somersaulting, changing from one paw to the other. The men coax her with bits of steak, the women with Portuguese endearments. Evva ignores them. The sight of the monkey upsets Annie. On a chain. She cuts into a slice of steak; bites, chews.

There is excited chatter. Annie and Francisco look up to see everyone watching the monkey head for Carlos. Evva runs up his arm, perches on his shoulder, grabs his face between her hairy little paws to kiss him on the mouth. Everyone laughs except Annie. Marcia says the monkey has never done this before, taken to a stranger.

Annie frowns. Francisco reaches over with more wine. Their eyes meet as he fills her glass. Carlos watches them, but the monkey is perched on his shoulder, a possessive little arm around his neck. The monkey has put him into the center of things.

The Brazilians laugh. They tease Annie about her rival and ask Carlos what his secret is.

Annie answers. "Carlos has no secret. The monkey is on a chain. Carlos just happens to be there." Then she asks Francisco, "Why don't you set the poor thing free?"

Francisco says, "It must be chained. It might run away.

Or someone might steal it."

The monkey scampers back to her avocado tree, chain clanging on the clothes line as she climbs, runs.

One of the men brings out a guitar and Francisco picks up his *cavalcino*. As they strum together, Annie relaxes. Wine has made her sentimental. The first Portuguese she learned had been words to songs sung at parties. She asks them to play *Fernando*, and they all sing.

Agora a hora está chegando. The hour is arriving. About parting. As always, there is argument about whether the Argentinians stole the song from Brazilians, or vice versa. Annie knew it in Canada as *Cielito Lindo, Beautiful Heaven*.

She wants to leave before she cries. She signals Carlos across the room.

Francisco's awareness of her is disturbing. He watches her, he knows. She must get away. What are the rules for flirtation here? She's a newlywed. Men tease her, but she has not been a target of the usual Brazilian overtures.

Carlos is enjoying himself. He liked the attention he got because of the monkey and would like to stay. He better not push his luck with me tonight, Annie thinks. She strides across the patio. "Let's go. Now. " She knows that he will not make a scene here. It would spoil his act.

He drapes his heavy arm around her shoulder and leads her across the patio to make farewells. Forcing a smile, she embraces and kisses cheeks. Francisco lingers when he kisses her; his *abraço* a little too long. He keeps his arm on her shoulder as he and Marcia walk them to the door.

In the car, she sings the sad Portuguese song. It is silent when they pass *O Caminho ao Céu*. It is dark, except for one light at the back. Moonlight shines on rows of coffins.

Before, on the way home from parties, Annie always

held Carlos's hand and grasped it tightly, felt mellow and reconciled after all the fun, wine and food.

She could do this tonight. Just reach out to hold his hand. Her gesture would please Carlos.

It would make everything better if she did.

She clasps her hands together and rests them on her lap. And she hums.

A Bouquet of Roses

Annie walks up the hill to a fashion show for the mothers' group at the church hall. Olive and Martha, her missionary friends, have insisted that she attend this event. The church is a big white building with colored lights that nightly spell *IGREJA EVANGELICA*. She can see it now, on the crest of the hill as she trudges on in the heat, wishing she had never got into this. She dislikes this particular church because poor Brazilians see its blazing neon lights as some kind of miracle. They light their own homes with crude lamps made of tins picked from garbage cans. These tins, their origins blatant — *pasta de tomate, oleo Mazola*, are stuffed with cotton wicks and filled with oil. They are admired by the rich in art galleries down south in Rio, and by foreign wives in markets up here in the Northeast. The lamps are so touching, so frugal, Annie thinks, and so damned pathetic. She has bought several of these tin-crafted objects — a big bowl that she uses for fruit and a couple of little lamps. Souvenirs from my travels, she thinks, to show off back in Canada. I'm as big a hypocrite as everyone else.

She shifts her shoulder bag to the other arm. The bag is heavy, damp with sweat. Why, she wonders, did I get caught up in this? I don't know anyone in the mothers' group but I try to fit in and I'm afraid of offending Martha and Olive. The social worker in me, I guess. Social workers are really sort of missionaries, when it comes down to it.

Annie had met the two women a few weeks after arriving in Lagoa Grande, after she finally persuaded Carlos to let her shop at the market instead of sending Fatima, their maid. He had protested. "I don't want my wife seen wandering around town alone. It's important to make a good impression. Tim Manning's wife goes to the Hyperbompreco. Why don't you give her a call?"

"If I was crazy about supermarkets, I'd have stayed in Canada. Vicky Manning isn't even learning Portuguese. What kind of impression does that make?"

Reluctantly, Carlos conceded.

Annie had set out on foot, another habit that makes her appear eccentric. Vicky Manning told her this was dangerous. "You never know what might happen, Annie. I only step out of the car to pick up the mail. I can't stand the streets. We just aren't used to seeing that kind of poverty in Canada."

"Oh, no?" Annie had retorted. "Ever been up North, visited a Native reserve?"

"That's different. I hope nothing bad happens to you, Annie. The way you wander around alone."

Annie had loved her first sight of the market and been dazzled, strolling among stalls. The noise, the color. Stall-keepers called out, brilliant-colored parrots screamed, monkeys chattered in cages.

It had felt exciting and unreal — as if she had walked into a foreign film without subtitles. Wandering from stall to stall just looking around she had enjoyed herself so much that she forgot her shopping list. Raw meat and sausages hung from hooks; pineapples, mangoes and other exotic fruits she could not identify tumbled over bins.

All the strangeness — unfamiliar produce, language, money. The heat, the sun, the sweat, had been too much for her.

She wished that she could just turn around and go home. Carlos would gloat. She could hear him say, "See? You should have listened to me." He would smile, shake his head and say, "I told you, Annie!"

She braced herself, leaning one arm against a stall. Sweat poured down her forehead and blurred her eyes. What to do? she wondered. I'll just buy the first thing I see and get the hell out. Scared and frantic, she looked for produce that she recognized and knew the Portuguese words for. She saw a bin of potatoes, pointed and murmured, "*Batatas inglesas.*" A cheroot-smoking woman counted out several potatoes, looked up and asked, "*Basta?*"

"*Sim,*" Annie answered. After she had taken out her wallet and paid, a manicured white hand closed over hers. Startled, she turned and faced two women.

"Don't show your money like that. You'll have people following you. I'm Olive Herman," the woman drawled. "My husband is pastor of the American Mission." She was pale and blonde. "This is Martha Jackson. Her husband is the other pastor. We're from Alabama."

Martha was tall and brown-haired. Neither woman was tanned. Martha spoke. "You must be with that new bunch of Canadians who just arrived. If we can help, we'd be glad to. You're brave, tackling the market. Canadian wives usually don't come here. But it's the best place to shop."

"I'm Annie da Silva. I'm so relieved to meet you!"

The two women exchanged knowing smiles.

"The heat, the crowd . . . I was frantic. You rescued me just in time!"

"It's hard, at first, down here in Brazil," Olive said. "You just need someone to show you around and explain things and you'll be fine. We've been here fifteen years and still remember how scary things seem at first."

Annie let them take over, trailing after them and listening as they showed her how to bargain. They told her how to prepare tropical fruits and vegetables and impressed upon her the need to insist that her maid wash produce to remove parasites.

"You have to watch them like a hawk, the maids," Olive said. "They get careless. They're just not used to living the way we do."

Annie frowned. "Not Fatima! She's been wonderful. I'd never have made it through those first weeks without her, I was so homesick. She sat beside me while I showed her pictures of my family. She was my first friend here."

Olive and Martha exchanged glances. "You don't need to do that any more, you hear?" Martha said, "You've got us now."

"Martha's right," Olive continued. "Now, don't take offence, but that's a problem you Canadians have here. Spoiling the maids. You mustn't consider Fatima a friend or she'll take advantage. That's not fair to her. She'll never fit in after you've gone if you treat her as an equal."

Annie kept quiet. After all, the women had rescued her and they were kind and friendly. Grateful, she accepted their offer of a lift home. She admired their fluency in Portuguese and their know-how as they summoned a boy to carry purchases to their station wagon. She stared in wonder as the child hoisted an enormous fruit-laden basket on his head and swaggered off.

They answered her questions about social problems.

Yes, there was a drought in this area. Yes, gastroenteritis was a killer of infants. Starvation? They didn't know the statistics.

"The main problem here is that folks haven't found the Lord. We're not social reformers, we're here to preach the gospel."

"But surely there are practical things to be done." Annie suggested.

"Well, yes. We help folks in our congregation who have been saved. Why, we've a project for the mothers, the poor ones, to use sewing machines at the church. Folks from up home send money for fabric so they can make clothes for their children."

Despite her disagreements with the missionaries, Annie thought that they could provide her with a way to get involved and get to know the real Brazil. She'd been uncomfortable with all the new luxuries — a maid, free housing, a living allowance.

She had wondered what she could do to be useful. She couldn't sew, but she could make donations to show her gratitude, to give something back. Having been a social worker probably exaggerated her North American compulsion to fix everything, especially people. Here, she had been relieved to see an acceptance and appreciation of imperfection. In the wonderful, irregular clay pots she bought from street peddlers; in the way the blind, crippled and crazy were out on the streets, not tucked away in institutions the way they used to be in Canada.

Worry lines had left her forehead. She had time to herself. Time to swim, to read. Her husband's lab assistant, Marcus, had commented on her changed appearance. She even understood him when he told her in Portuguese that she walked easy and loose, like a Brazilian woman. Sometimes she sang, her voice joining those of maids in the building as they ironed, swept, laundered. So much music here: so much pain.

All she had to do was amuse herself. She went swimming among hibiscus petals and drank beer at the Clube Campestre; napped, studied Portuguese and wrote colorful letters home. There is no work with deprived families and their late night emergencies. In Toronto, she would have been able to be useful; here, she sees worse deprivation and is agonized to see beggars, homeless little kids wandering the streets, makeshift shanties that many people live in. But she has no base, no structure from which to help.

When she discussed her concern with Carlos, he had exploded. "I saved you from that! Why can't you appreciate this new life I've given you?"

She did appreciate it. At first. The parties and dressing up to go out with other Canadians. It was romantic and exciting, but after a while it seemed wrong. We're supposed to be providing foreign aid here, she thought, yet we're living more extravagantly than we did in Canada. At parties, Annie noticed a group of Canadian professors that she called "career colonials." They traveled from contract to contract, from third-world country to third-world country, and compared servants in Jamaica to maids in Colombia or Haiti, housing in India to that in Brazil. It was tempting, she felt the lure herself. Adventure, luxury, subsidized travel. But her profession and politics nudged her into discomfort. An unease that was another thing she could not share with Carlos. He was already scouting other contracts in Brazil and talked of using their savings to open an electronics factory and become a Brazilian millionaire.

He was angry when she did not share his enthusiasm.

To Annie, it didn't seemed fair for them to be privileged when there was such need in the country around them. So she kept in touch with Olive and Martha, and every month after Carlos received his check, she gave them two or three hundred *cruzeiros* for fabric and thread. Conscience money.

She argued with the two women during their attempts to discuss her religious affiliations and beliefs, but read the Bible with them weekday afternoons because it was a relief to speak English again. The missionaries were upset that she did not believe in the devil and would not attend their church, but when they asked her to visit the poor and sick of the congregation, she jumped at the opportunity. This was more like it! She would not be another gringo, she would know the real Brazil. The church group was a start. When her Portuguese improved and she knew her way around and made friends among Brazilians, she would get involved on her own.

Every week she got into the missionaries' big station wagon and was driven off with the church ladies to bring groceries to people who lived in dirt-floored, tin-roofed shanties. While Martha and Olive spoke of the weather and the Lord, Annie left food in the kitchen. Then, late in the afternoon, the group drove to homes where prayers were showered on the wealthy ill who lived in stone-walled, iron-gated mansions with swimming pools. After prayers, maids brought cups of sweet strong coffee and showed them through the houses. All the rooms, all the heavy imported furniture.

Sometimes her disagreement with the women irritated her and she pulled away until one of them called and invited her to join them and try out new recipes. She would give in, go along to their homes and have fun poring over cookbooks with them.

Near the church Annie passes boys carrying fruit-laden baskets on their heads, women clutching babies to their breasts. Sticky smells of chocolate, coffee and cane liquor assail her from stalls.

Olive and Martha wait at the church entrance. They smile as they flutter out to greet her. Their behavior worries her. She is not important and her attendance should not be so significant. Olive ushers her over to meet *Dona* Amelia Gonçalves, president of the Ladies' Auxiliary. *Dona* Amelia is tall, blonde, composed and dressed too elegantly for this event. Olive and Martha always wear printed cotton house dresses — a habit Annie likes about them. They share the simple habit of rural Canadian housewives. *Dona* Amelia is not the type usually encountered in Paraiba. One look at her and Annie feels uneasy and decides: back in Toronto, Rosedale. Here, Rio. *Dona* Amelia must have come from some big luxury apartment along Guinle Park.

Dona Amelia smiles a polite smile and places a cool kiss on Annie's cheeks. Annie is not surprised that when *Dona* Amelia speaks, she hears the melodic accent of south Brazil. The trilled r's, the almost Spanish pronunciation. Not the speech of a *Nordestina*. This could be interesting, she thinks. Even Olive and Martha appear edgy as they usher her into the hall where the tea and fashion show will be held.

Women from the church visitors group recognize Annie and single her out. Mothers from the sewing group, the poor mothers, cluster around her asking questions. Because they are dark skinned, Annie is glad of her tan, it helps her feel less foreign. Olive, Martha and *Dona* Amelia, carefully pale, stand out.

Annie speaks her set piece in Portuguese.

"I have been here six months. Yes, I like it very much. I love the climate. No, I enjoy the heat. I especially like your tropical fruits. No, we have no mangoes in Canada. Yes, we have much snow. No, I have never seen an Eskimo. I have one daughter and one son. Yes, they are both married."

Olive and Martha smile with approval at her performance. Annie feels like a prize catch.

Dona Amelia plays the organ softly. At this cue, people sit on folding chairs. Annie joins the mothers, their faces lit with expectant smiles. A girl from the youth group walks to the microphone and announces the beginning of the fashion show. Excited, the mothers stir in their seats. The girl calls each child by name and describes the garment she models. A jacket and skirt for church, a dress for birthday parties, slacks and top for play. One by one, the little models walk across the stage, giggling with embarrassment and pride.

Annie is distressed because she knows that these are the only clothes the children will have this year. And next, and the next. She is uncomfortable and sad, afraid to look around.

Everyone claps with enthusiasm. Especially the mothers, in frayed dresses carefully bleached and ironed for today.

Dona Amelia takes the microphone. The clapping stops, the audience listens. Olive and Martha beam their white smiles.

Dona Amelia wears an elegant blue sheath dress. Annie recognizes it as *labyrynthine*, lacy drawn-work.

Canadians drive to Fortaleza in Northern Brazil to buy lace and these finely crafted gowns.

Dona Amelia's long dramatic speech lends prestige to the occasion. The mothers sit up straight, their faces serious as she reports how much fabric has been purchased and how many hours the mothers have spent sewing.

She smiles as she refers to a benefactor whose generosity made this great event possible. "For all the endeavor we have admired today, we must thank a visitor, a new friend of Brazil . . ."

As the drift of the speech dawns on Annie, stunned, she pretends not to understand. She looks for an exit, an out.

". . . and a friend of our church, *Dona* Annie Da Silva!"

Annie looks at Olive and Martha. Then, triumphant, they smile.

When *Dona* Amelia summons her onto the stage, Annie shakes her head. Disapproval flashes across *Dona* Amelia's face. She sees the foreigner's uneasiness, disappearing smile. She beckons again.

Dazed, Annie complies. *Dona* Amelia possesses the poise of the rich; Annie does not. The dark smiling faces of mothers and children blur before her. *Dona* Amelia nods, gestures a signal. Two little girls walk on the stage carrying an enormous bouquet of roses. Expensive yellow roses from a florist, which they present to Annie.

Everyone smiles expectantly.

They want something from me, Annie thinks. A speech? A smile? Everyone is proud and happy now. Except me, because I was just told that I'm responsible for all the joy here today.

She cannot smile the benevolent smile which the dark faces and *Dona* Amelia expect.

She frowns, her body stiffens because she knows that the cost of these roses could buy a month's supply of fabric for the mothers. She pulls herself together, mumbles thanks and strains to smile for the audience. At *Dona* Amelia's urging, she follows the children off the stage.

Olive and Martha rush over to *Dona* Amelia and whisper. *Dona* Amelia apologizes to the audience and tells them that Annie does not understand the language. Annie fumbles and says in Portuguese that the flowers were so beautiful that she was overcome. She hates herself for lying, for going along with a charade.

She knows that under their smiles, the people here have found her out. She has failed to act her part and has disappointed everyone. She's just another foreigner who does not know the rules here, or knows them but does not like them. Now, she'll never to fit in. This presentation was supposed to be the climax of today's event, a coup for Olive and Martha.

Annie makes the obligatory round of cheek-kissing, darts to the door and leaves. *Dona* Amelia, Olive and Martha are all smiles, but do not protest her abrupt departure. The mothers' eyes follow her, bewildered.

Annie feels that she has lost her one hope for being useful, for being more than a foreign intruder.

Carlos would not understand, she can't tell him of today's fiasco. He would just give her another lecture on the need to accept things here as they are. She has never felt so alone, so confused.

She hunches her shoulders and walks slowly downhill toward the new white apartment building reserved for foreign professors. In front of it, a beggar rummages in the garbage, hiding discarded bread under her shawl.

Annie cringes in the shadow of the building with the expensive roses as she tries to avoid passing the woman.

The beggar turns around, and seeing the roses, breaks into a marvelous toothless smile.

Green and Gold

Heat assaults Jane as she and David near the plane's exit. When she looks out and sees palm trees, she no longer feels disappointed about missing her med school graduation ceremony to visit her parents in Brazil. She had struggled with the conflict and resisted her need for ritual and recognition.

Graduation was a farce anyway. Middle-class sham, David says.

"Thank you for flying Varig." The stewardess smiles her perfect smile, opens wide her green-lidded eyes.

"Thank you." Jane and David descend the staircase, swept again by gusts of heat as they search for her parents among a group of people waiting on the tarmac.

Back in Edmonton several months ago, her mother had phoned and cried, "I don't want to go to Brazil. I'm too old to pull up roots. I'll feel trapped. And Dr Jacobson said the climate would aggravate my arthritis."

Jane had winced. Always "my arthritis." Like a prize possession. She listens for this in patients. "My high blood pressure," and even, dear God, "my cancer." A clue that prognosis is poor. The patient has claimed the illness. Owns it.

After that phone call Jane had taken her mother out for lunch to talk. Over the years she had learned that her father's foreign contracts were often a geographic conclusion to an affair. Universities are small towns. Gossip gets around. Her mother either never heard about these affairs or, more likely, she did know but never let on.

"You don't have to stay down there, Mom. Go with Dad for a visit. Give it a try to find out if you like it or not."

"I have to decide right away so the university can arrange for our accommodation. If I go, I'll have to decide what to do about the house, ship all our things . . ."

"You might get depressed, away from your friends, away from us. But hang in for a while. You'll be shocked at first. Northeast Brazil is a bad area, David says. The poverty — "

"I know what David says. David knows everything."

Dammit, Jane thought. Try again. "Mom, do me a favor. If you go, take enough money for a return flight so you won't feel trapped. You don't have to tell Dad about it, but it will give you freedom of choice."

"I'd hate to keep anything from your father. It would be like lying."

Jane sighed. Although her mother irritated her, her simple honesty touched her.

After her parents had left for Brazil, Jane was relieved to see a withdrawal from an account to which she had access. Mom's savings from teaching. Jane knew that her father would cut his usual swath because even at sixty, he was still too damned handsome. Silver-white hair, blue eyes, ski-tanned face and something intense, athletic and young about the way he moved. Not much skiing near the equator, Jane thought, maybe he'll have to stay home more.

Her mother's letters were *too* happy. Brazil was beautiful, beautiful. She wrote about the luxuries of a maid, siestas, a country club. "I get to meet nice Brazilians who invite me to their homes to teach English. A dear Dutch boy visits me and we talk about farming in Alberta. You'd just love him. The Brazilians took to your dad right away. He fits right in. You should just hear him speak Portuguese."

Yeah, Jane thought, he fits in alright. Poor Mom.

When her mother had offered to pay for a flight to Brazil for a graduation gift, Jane knew she must visit. With David. How to persuade him? "Mom's getting on," she tried. "And you know Dad. I've got to go. Would you come with me?"

"Sure thing. That was great of Jessie."

His consent surprised her. He wasn't crazy about her parents, especially her father. She understood his enthusiasm when he explained, "Lagoa Grande is near Recife. Dom Camaro country. Liberation theology. We'll see what's up."

Jane sees her parents and waves. Her mother, red-faced and perspiring, is stuffed into a tight print dress. When Jane hugs her, her mother bursts into tears. Her father, in loose shirt and light slacks, is tanned and cool-looking. He shakes hands with David, asks, "How was the flight?"

"Good to see you, Malcolm." David nods to his father-in-law. "The flight was impressive. Waiting at Belem Airport was pure Graham Greene! It was so hot we saw steam rising from the jungle. I got a fantastic shot of the Amazon from the plane." David embraces her mother. "Hi there, Jessie."

"Graham Greene, eh?" Malcolm says. "We must go back that way. Rio is Montreal with a beach."

Her mother moves out of David's hug to clutch Jane. "You look so nice. Professional."

Nice. Professional. So much for the new dress, Jane thinks.

Her father kisses Jane's forehead, grasps her shoulders and says, "Janie, your hair's too short. Lady doctors!"

Jane shrugs, thinks, I'll never please him. What else is new?

They follow her father through the crowd to a big white car with a maple leaf logo on the side.

"Canadian government," her mother says. On the drive to Lagoa Grande, Jane and her mother clutch sweaty hands in the back seat; David and her dad chat in front. Jane sits up, keen at the sight of sun shimmering on the road, thatched huts in the *sertao*. She smiles and squeezes her mother's hand when they pass naked kids along the roadside. A little boy pees in the ditch.

"It's just like North Africa," David says.

There he goes, Jane thinks, talking about his travels. Europe, India. She smiles. She'd stayed home and traveled on chemical trips more interesting than David's. But those were never discussed. Not by a doctor.

"Dave, you're like all the other foreigners," her dad says. "They see Paraiba and compare it to Ontario, B.C. or Texas. Right, Jess?"

Jane knows her father puts David down because he disapproves of him. And of her. "Why can't you get real jobs?" he asks. "After all that money I spent on medical school. It's 'Native people' this and 'Aboriginal people' that. When I was a boy we called them Indians. They're still Indians."

Jessie says, "It's like the foothills near Lagoa. It'll remind you of Alberta, Jane."

"See what I mean?" Malcolm nudges David.

Although tired from the long hot flight, Jane revives. Her eyes shine at the sight of miles of sugar cane, women washing clothes in a pond, a naked little kid on a burro; of Brahma cattle grazing in blue-green pastures, and of palms forming green tunnels over the road. It's not so bad here after all, she decides. I came out of concern for Mom, but it could be fun. She hugs her mom and exclaims, "This is so exciting!"

Jessie beams. "I'm glad. You need a change after working so hard. My little girl, a doctor! Imagine that. I'm so proud. It was nice that David could come, too."

Her father interrupts, "We're nearing our watering hole. It's about midway and breaks the drive." He parks at a bus station, gets out and leads them into an open restaurant, striding ahead to claim a table, pushing his tall frame through a group of short Brazilians.

Jane observes faces. Wonderful faces. Mixed; African, Indian, Portuguese. The faces turn from the counter to smile at them. Jane and David smile back.

"Friendly people," David says.

"*Cuatros Antarcticas*," Malcolm commands.

Jane smirks, watching her father. Imperious. Presence, he's got it. Could claim the earth was flat and have a following. Of women. A waiter scurries to their table, sets down bottles and glasses. The men pour. Thirsty, they all drink, wordless for a while.

David says, "Look, Jane." He peels a label off the damp beer bottle. "See the trademark? A penguin. Antarctica. We're closer to it down here. "

"Another for your wonderful international collection."

His smile vanishes as he flattens the label on the plastic tabletop.

"Brahma Chopp is another good beer," her dad says. "*Chopp* is draft. A light pilsener. I've gone native — for me it's *cachaca* — a rough cane liquor the locals drink. We'll have *batidas* at our party next week. That's *cachaca* and passion-fruit juice. Jess, did you tell Jane about the party?"

"No, I didn't know if it was on for sure."

"It's on," he says.

Jane wants to hit him.

Her mother asks, "Did you bring a long dress, dear?"

"One of my Indian prints."

"Oh, no! Not one of those old hippie things? I meant a *nice* dress."

"I love it. It's cotton. Cool. Great for this climate. I didn't expect formality."

"Our handbook advised us to bring long dresses for parties. I've had Lucia — a dressmaker here — run some up."

"How colonial. Just like the good old days. The British in India." Her mother's face falls.

As soon as they arrive in Lagoa Seca her parents complain about people spitting on sidewalks; about beggars, drunks, sick people. David looks out and winces. Get used to it, David, Jane thinks, it's a lot like where we're going in northern Ontario.

After they settle in, they pass days reading, visiting craft markets and swimming at the Clube Campestre where Jane notices her mother's tan and thinks it makes her look like a big leather purse.

Jane enjoys the pool and the sun in a one-piece blue suit, but envies Brazilian women, not just their bikinis, but their way of moving proudly regardless of weight or age. *Maybe a yellow string bikini?*

She worries because her mother only enters the pool to cool off between drinks. And she drinks too much.

"You should swim lengths, Mom. A little exercise will help your joints."

"I'm not so sure, dear. I just listen to my body." A familiar line. Beverly's line. A vegetarian, Jane's sister has committed her life to skiing and working part-time as a waitress in Banff. She is her dad's favorite. He sends Beverly money to support her go-with-the-body lifestyle, but refuses to loan anything to Jane to set up practice with the Native People.

Her mother prepares for the party and nervously phones to invite people. The Mannings, the Clarks, the Gagnons from Quebec. "You can practice your French, David."

A few days earlier, she had dragged Jane to a beauty salon. To her surprise, Jane had fun. The two giggled together, getting manicures and pedicures, picking out nail polish colors.

Jane had been surprised at her mother's proficiency in Portuguese as she chatted with the manicurist, the hairdressers. Mom will be okay here, Jane decides. She is holding her own.

Jane dreads the party and is relieved when the day arrives. Her parents' maid, Geralda, makes snacks, spearing cubes of cheese with toothpicks. Jane bakes her favorite hippy carrot cake. Minus mood-altering herbs. When Jane, working from David's Portuguese dictionary, announces, "*Um bolo do cenoura*," as she slathers the top with cream cheese icing, Geralda giggles at the idea of carrots and cheese, in cake.

The cake is a triumph. Aside from that, Jane finds the party an ordeal. The guests are five Canadian couples, several young Brazilians and her father's assistant, Manuela — a small dark beauty in a strapless white dress with a bare panel exposing her flat brown belly. Manuela passes drinks and canapes as if she were the hostess. Jessie knocks back gin-and-tonic. Three Brazilian girls question Jane in careful English. They are accompanying husbands to Canada on exchange programs and have assumed their own automatic acceptance into med schools. Lots of luck, Jane thinks.

The party would have been agony without Hans, a Dutch agronomist, her mother's friend. Dark and stocky, warm and friendly, he seems fond of her mom. He is fluent in English. Jane likes him and is pleased that he and David hit it off. He invites them to a *cooperativo*, where he works with Redemptorist priests, and to a hospital improvised by a Belgian doctor-priest who takes care of the poor. Jane is relieved. David was getting edgy. He was disappointed at not learning about what was going on politically in the region. She is excited about the invitation. She might learn something here.

She smiles, nods, circulates and avoids Manuela, who tries to get chummy. Jane yawns at Manuela's perpetual smile and chatter.

Early in the morning, guests straggle out. When they have all left, her mother hugs her. "It was a great success! Everyone loved you. There will be more parties for you and David. Brazilians are like that."

"No. I'm not up for more parties."

Her mother smiles. "We'll see."

Malcolm and David sip a nightcap of Chivas Regal.

"Hans is great," David says. "Those priests sound interesting."

"They're interesting all right," Malcolm blurts. "Under police surveillance. They're troublemakers. You're not going to visit any goddamn priests."

"Malcolm's right, David. *Dona* Marcia Figuierido, my English pupil, says we shouldn't."

Jane says. "We're still going to that hospital."

"Not with me. Not in our car," her father announces. "I've a job to consider. Somebody in this family has to earn a living."

Tell that to Beverly, Jane thinks.

"I'm considering *my* job," she asserts. "This doctor-priest can probably give me better ideas for my practice up North than I'll learn interning in Edmonton hospitals." She traces her finger around the wild print of the Indian skirt. Patchouli scent clings, despite the years and the maid Geralda's loving hand-washing. *Vancouver. Making candles that summer. My first time in the ocean. Mountains. Mom's lucky to have Geralda. I'll leave the dress for Geralda.*

"Well, I'm not going," her father announces, "and you're not taking our car."

"But Malcolm," her mother pleads, "it should be all right. The Canadian presence among the poor. Showing that we care."

"I don't want that car seen out there," he commands.

The next day Hans averts a crisis. He phones and offers a Jeep more suited to the rough terrain.

Jessie is relieved when Zé, the driver, stops the Jeep. Thank God, she thinks. That little Brazilian was either deliberately trying to scare me or else he just enjoyed being in the driver's seat. The Jeep saved the day, thanks to Hans. He's like a son, dropping in on Sundays when Geralda is off and Malcolm is out working at the university. Sundays would be awful without Hans.

Hans helps her out of the Jeep, shakes hands with Zé,

tells him, "*O mismo como Fittipaldi.*" They all laugh. Jessie smooths her sticky cotton skirt, stretches her aching knees and rubs a pain in her back. She looks around and see piles of bricks near a church, several small new homes and more bricks stacked near half-finished walls. A tall, lean man strides from the church to greet them. Jessie observes his plaid shirt and jeans; his cropped gray hair and bright blue eyes behind steel-rimmed glasses. She is immediately taken with him and thinks that he looks just like Paul Newman, except for the glasses. The priest nods to them, then, frowning, speaks to Hans in Dutch before he waves at them and hurries off.

"He apologizes for leaving," Hans explains. "He has to go to Recife. Two priests there have been jailed, so he's gone to try and get them out. They were begging bread from rich people and distributing it to petty thieves and whores at street Masses. Someone in Brasilia calls this Communism."

Jessie is disappointed that the good-looking priest has gone. And confused. Brasilia is such a nice clean city, the capital. The nicest place she has visited in Brazil. People there must know what they are doing. She is pleased, though, to follow Hans and David, to have Jane beside her and to leave Zé, that crazy little driver. Like a child with a toy, behind the wheel. Such a short man. No wonder people here adore Malcolm. Because he is tall. *Nordestino* men are so slight.

They reach a rambling, one-story building surrounded by coconut palms, guava, papaya and avocado trees. Jessie can identify them all because when she can't sleep at night, she reads up on tropical fruits, plants and flowers. Hans rings the bell.

Jessie pushes aside a branch of flaming jacarandas. When she hears hummingbirds, she nudges David. "The Portuguese word for hummingbird is *besaflor*, David. That means 'flower-kisser.' Isn't that cute?"

"Nice, " he acknowledges. He smiles a moment, then turns away to continue talking to Hans.

Some linguist, Jessie thinks. She turns to her daughter and whispers, "You know, Jane, if I were really ill, I'd have no hesitation about coming out to see this Dr Ahermaa. The priest-doctor? Or whatever. Even Dona Marcia, my English pupil, speaks highly of him. Her own husband is a doctor. He and the other doctors consult this priest all the time on the q.t. All he asks for in return are antibiotic samples. Brazilian specialists expect the skies. He'll even settle for a bottle of cognac. They say he's a drinker. I wish you'd let me bring that bottle of cognac as a friendly gesture. Here they call it '*cognac-i*.' Got to put an vowel on the end of everything."

When Jessie sees Jane set her lips, she knows that her daughter is angry and is holding something back. About what? My mentioning cognac? She keeps at me about drinking. But then, she's always been moody. Always. She looks so young with her hair cut short. It still curls tightly in the heat. Like when she was little. I could never get a brush through it.

She reaches out, touches Jane's hair and says, "My friend *Dona* Marcia speaks English very well. She studied for years with Americans at the Yazigi Institute. She practices with me because she thinks that Canadian accents are nicer. I'm flattered. It's a real break, socially. Dona Marcia knows everything and everybody in Lagoa Grande."

Jessie feels weepy. Jane isn't even listening. Here she is, trying to get close to her daughter and being ignored. She's hurt because of David's indifference, because the nice-looking priest left, and because the heat makes her feel weepy. So do Brazilians.

Like Dona Marcia and that transaction last week. Twenty-five *cruzeiros* to the dollar. Bobby Jean from the American mission got thirty in Recife at the black market in that seedy little hotel, The Galicia.

All Dona Marcia really wanted from me was dollars, she thinks. I thought she was my only friend, besides Hans. Canada? Go back? No. Husbands not safe in Northeast Brazil. Patricia, the coordinator, warned me. Eight women to each man. Aggressive Brazilian women. Whispers of broken marriages, of wives whisked home, husbands' contracts extended.

Malcolm even told me the first question put to him by Manuela. "Are you married?" Then, "Did your wife accompany you?"

Finally, "Does she like it here?"

He had chuckled. "These girls are so desperate they'll settle for any arrangement."

Last week he told me that I should go back with Jane to escape the rainy season.

No, dammit. I'm staying, arthritis or no arthritis.

Zé dusts seats, the dashboard. Car. Driving. Power. Going to town with Hans. Buying faucets, hoses. Beer with Hans in Lagoa. Like a friend. What's the catch? I gave him girls' names. Hans says no, his own girl is coming from Holland. Like priests? No, Hans just different. Lives with us, not with the *tecnicos* in Gringo Palace.

Zé lights a cigarette from a pack given to him by Father van Geffen. What guys, those *Redemptoristas*. The brick *cooperativo*. Our own houses. Better than before, in huts made of cartons, at the edge of the da Sousas', depending on leftover food sneaked out by maids. Soon lots of beans from the rigged-up irrigation that Hans helped us build.

Zé smiles as he gives the back seat a swipe with the cloth. The da Sousa family put up big signs forbidding people to pick fruit. A joke. Most people can't read. Who needs to? In Lagoa, things get around. Father van Geffen visited the da Sousas and asked for oranges that would go to waste. They gave him a basketful. That day. Later, they joined the big new church, the other one, run by Americans. Gave them money for electric guitars, fancy colored lights.

Religion. What is it? Priests? They work with us, make bricks. Fix the land, grow beans, dry them. Make a pond for fish. Houses, beans, fish.

These Canadian kids. The little girl pretty, but too sad. Her husband short, dark, like a *Brasileiro*. Hans tried to explain what he does. Helps the Indians get back their land. They have lost their land? I am proud of my Indian blood. My father, Moacir, was Indian. I thought in Canada there were those other people, Eskimos, who live in ice houses.

Dona Jessie. Poor old fat lady. Zé flicks a rag across the hood. Nothing wrong with fat. He likes his women fat. Young ones. It's the way she bulges. Tight dresses. She wanted to bring the fancy white car with the red leaf on the door. People thought it belonged to a big shot tobacco salesman, but this leaf is from some tree in Canada. Crazy.

Zé chuckles, spits on the cloth, polishes door handles. Professor Malcolm parks the car right in front of Manuela's every Sunday afternoon. Lucky guy, laying Manuela. She is beautiful, a jewel. Professor Malcolm fits right in. *A bem Brasileiro.*

Speeding around the corners high in the Barbaremas, Zé had smiled. The terror in Dona Jessie's eyes, her gray hair flying.

Jessie wipes sweat from her face with a fresh linen handkerchief. Hans knocks on the hospital door and a tired-looking man greets them. He is white-haired, balding; cheeks grizzled as though he hasn't shaved. He wears a shirt loose over dark pants. What kind of doctor is this? Jessie wonders. He embraces Hans but is unsmiling during introductions. A stern man.

Chatter. About the language of operation? Yes. David understands a bit of everything. When he interrupts in French, Dr Ahermaa's face brightens. He looks at David and obviously approves of him. Why? Because of his French? His enthusiasm? His beard? The beard. Like Ché Guevara. Radicals always recognize each other. Like homosexuals.

Speaking French, David seems like a new person, is less earnest, his face and gestures are animated. He looks just like the French in Quebec. Malcolm had taken her to Montreal on their honeymoon. It had been her first trip away from Alberta and she'd been homesick the whole time. Even then, Malcolm tried to fit it by speaking French. She'd felt left out from the very beginning.

Jessie wonders, Why do people change when speaking a foreign language? Malcolm is a stranger, speaking Portuguese at parties. He smiles, touches people, waves his arms. Speaking English, he is dignified, controlled. Hers.

David breaks into English and says, "The police raided just last week. They do this once a month. They don't like to because they're Catholic. The last time they had to raid during some kind of an epidemic. Two babies had just died and their families were crying."

Jessie stiffens. She'd glimpsed a row of coffins in a storage room off the corridor. That's the worst thing about Northeast Brazil. Coffins everywhere. At home, thank God, they're out of sight.

Soon David and the doctor are so involved in French discussion that David forgets to interpret until he has some real gem. Then his face lights up and he blurts. "He says he came here from the Belgian Congo!"

Jane fidgets, interrupts. "I want to see his set-up. Could we please get on with it?"

David translates and the doctor walks ahead, beckons them to follow. At the end of a long corridor a black, short-haired dog sleeps near a window. Not really a window, just an opening in the wall. Sun beats on the dog's back. The animal twitches, disturbed by flies.

There are small wards off the corridor with three steel cots to a wall. Beside the cots, a table holds coconuts with straws in them. Another dog, a brown one, sleeps beside a patient's bed. Jessie watches the doctor speak to his patients and gently touch them through bleach-worn sheets. When she sees the coconuts, she remembers that drink in Acapulco. *Coco loco*? Or something. Tequila. Rum. Our twenty-fifth anniversary. I got a terrible sunburn and had to stay inside the whole time.

"Ask him about the dogs, David. And find out what's in the coconuts."

"They're allowed to bring their pets. Sometimes it's all

they have. That's coconut water in the coconuts. It's safe, free, grows on the grounds and contains nutrients. Besides, they believe in it and they can't afford bottled water."

"Oh." She nudges Jane. "Dogs? Isn't that unsanitary?"

"I like it. I think it's a good idea."

Fancy medical schools. Meet the patient's emotional needs and never mind the rabies. Or parasites. Dogs carry them and their fleas carry leishmaniasis, a tropical illness. Jessie read about this in a medical encyclopedia, boning up on tropical diseases.

"Look, Mom, the lab." Her daughter's face brightens. It is a tiny white room the size of her powder room back home. There are steel tables, shelves, microscopes, test tubes. Jars.

"It's perfect!" Jane enthuses. "Exactly what I want." Dr Ahermaa smiles and puts his arm around her. Priests and doctors get off on Jane. Her work, her heroic work and dedication; her bright, child's eyes. David has probably told Dr Ahermaa that they will live on a reserve without light or water. Jessie knows Jane is smiling because of Ahermaa's approval, and that because she needs it, she laps it up.

It wasn't Malcolm's fault that he and Jane never got along. He'd had to work hard and had been away a lot. Jane never tried to please him and was always too serious. Then all of a sudden taking off for Vancouver and going wild on drugs. Married to an Easterner and will move up North. Perhaps if she had skied like Beverly.

Jessie frowns, swats a fly.

David and Ahermaa continue in French, some of which Jane apparently understands. She nods, asks questions. When did she learn this? The priest says something and they laugh.

"What's going on?" Jessie asks.

Jane points to three jars of brown stuff. David chuckles and explains, "Dr Ahermaa calls it expensive shit. Rich people's from Lagoa Grande. He's an expert on intestinal parasites, so they consult him instead of their own doctors."

What kind of priest talks like that? Jessie wonders, and winces at the sight of his shaking nicotine-stained fingers. She, too, needs a drink.

They follow Ahermaa out of the lab, around a corner and into a dingy kitchen. It is cool, on the building's shady side.

"My liv-ing-room," Ahermaa sounds out carefully.

Jessie notices rows of empty cognac bottles under the sink. Ahermaa waves towards several rickety chairs.

After they all sit down, Ahermaa speaks to Hans, who explains,"He asked me to go and get the new Dutch volunteer. A nurse who arrived last week. We'll be right back."

Ahermaa opens a cupboard and takes out a bottle of cognac.

A little brown bird flies into the room, perches on a shelf and chirps. Jessie looks around. There are other birds in a wicker cage. And at the far end of the room in a metal cage is an enormous parrot, a green and gold macaw. Her encyclopaedia describes them as "gregarious but monogamous." These macaws are precious because they are an endangered species and because of their colors, the colors of Brazil. Jessie is excited about that because green and gold are also the colors of Alberta.

Ahermaa sees Jessie watching the parrot.

"Romeo," he says. As if recognizing its name, the parrot preens for her, flaunts his colors. He pauses on his perch and trains his bright beady eyes on her. As she stares back, smiling, she is reminded of the Rio carnival, of the flamboyant men. And also of the medical encyclopedia. Psittacosis. A deadly disease carried by parrots.

She shifts her bulky body on the small wooden chair to ease her joints. This is no country for girdles. What is Malcolm doing, home alone? Will he make sure that Geralda doesn't wreck tonight's roast chicken with cumin?

Why can't Ahermaa hurry up with the cognac? She watches him rip plastic, pull the cork and pour.

Hans returns and introduces Anna, a big Dutch girl. She smiles as she circles the group and shakes hands vigorously with everyone, then awkwardly rushes to help Ahermaa with the drinks.

Ahermaa brings a half-full tumbler to Jessie. She looks at her watch, at Jane. It's not even noon. It would be rude to refuse. Jane smirks. Ahermaa puts the glass firmly in Jessie's hand, looks her squarely in the eye and smiles. He clinks his tumbler against hers.

Anna passes drinks to the others. Smaller ones. She sits down and spreads her knees out, leaning over to stretch her long arms across the wide stiff skirt. She has freckles and frizzy auburn hair. Jessie decides she had been a farm girl before she became a nurse.

They chat in English, French, Portuguese, Dutch. The wild bird flies over to perch beside the caged ones.

Ahermaa smiles at Jessie as he tops her drink and his own.

The black dog wanders into the kitchen and plunks down at Jessie's feet, leaning against her leg. His weight is comforting to her. So is the cognac.

The young people smile, observing the wild bird and the caged ones checking each other out. Jessie and Ahermaa exchange glances. Dear Dr Ahermaa, Jessie thinks. Why, he's like an old friend. It's as though we've always known each other.

Together, they watch the parrot. She wishes now that she had learned French, so that she could really talk to Ahermaa. She wants to tell him that she wonders how the parrot feels, that she wonders what it feels like to be so extravagantly beautiful.

Cuba: Scent of Jasmine

Foreign Correspondent

Tourist

Foreign Correspondent

September, 1962

I should have worn my pink silk dress after all, Linda thinks, as she passes Africans in brightly colored batiks, Indians in Nehru jackets with their sari-clad wives. Back in Toronto, she had thought that her green shirtmaker dress made her look like a journalist, but she sees that it's the same color as Cuban militia uniforms. Now she feels nondescript for such a momentous event. Probably just as well.

A student in white blouse and navy skirt ushers her to the front. The girl's outfit worries Linda because it looks like a uniform, which suggests totalitarianism. The North American press could be right about Cuba. The girl directs her to an empty front row marked with a Canadian flag and a sign: *El Cuerpo Diplomatico do Canada*. At first, this prestigious seating thrills her, but after realizing that no Canadian diplomats are likely to show up, she feels edgy, as if fearing a Mountie will appear to pronounce her an imposter. Right now, a Mountie would be a relief: exhaustion and heat have heightened her imagination.

Can it only be last night that she slept in Toronto? She had boarded the Miami-bound plane long before dawn. Her first flight, first trip to a foreign country, first venture into journalism. Now that her daughter was older, she hopes to become a foreign correspondent and participate on TV panel discussions. The expert on Cuba.

For years she stayed home with her daughter while

her husband Earl, a mining engineer, flew all over world in search of metals. Once, he had kissed her goodbye and said, "Never mind. Maybe some day, you'll fly somewhere." With a pang she had watched his plane disappear while her daughter tugged at her, whimpering, "Daddy." It was always the same. Drive home. Feed Brenda. Bathe her, then read extra Dr Seuss stories to her in the hope of easing her longing for the exciting, important Daddy.

Here, seated in the Chaplin Theater in Havana waiting to hear a speech by Fidel Castro, she shivers with excitement, thinks, Now it's my turn.

She cannot believe her day as she pieces it together. Events are fragmented; a movie that began in the Miami airport when two Cubans came up to her, begging her to take serum to a sick child in Havana.

A short dark man asked, "You are *Señora* Campbell from Toronto?"

"Yes. I am *Señora* Campbell." She enjoyed identifying herself as *señora*, wrapped up in feeling deliciously worldly, she had never thought to wonder how they knew her name, how they could pick her out of the group waiting for the connection to Havana.

"Please, *Señora*, take this medicine to my wife! My little girl is dying of polio and needs this serum." The man held a small vial. Linda was confused. Polio? She had read that Cuba was the first country in the world to vaccinate all its citizens against polio with the new Sabine-Salk. The man grasped her shoulder.

If she challenged him, he would probably deny what she had read about health reforms. As the men raved in Spanish, she caught *enfermo, muerte*. What if what she had read was propaganda? Too hot and tired to argue, she reached for the bottle.

The dark man thrust it into her hand. "See this name and phone number?" He pointed to a label on the bottle. "It is my wife. Phone her. She will pick it up. Please, *Señora*, where are you staying?"

"At Havana Libre." Nothing had been confirmed, but that was where she intended to stay.

"*Gracias, gracias, Señora.* You will save my daughter!" Before she could ask further questions, the two men disappeared into the crowd.

Linda had slipped the bottle into her purse and felt annoyed and embarrassed. Annoyed because she wondered if she had been conned; embarrassed because the bottle looked like a urine specimen. But it was no big deal compared to the suitcase she had checked that contained enough clothes to last six weeks — the length of time she felt it would take her to learn all about the Russians and missile bases she had read about in Toronto newspapers. *10,000 RUSSIAN TROOPS LAND IN CUBA. U.S. FEARS INVASION.*

She had hoped to visit St Pierre and Miquelon for her first flight and perhaps become a travel writer. When she inquired about the French Islands, she learned that she would have to change planes three times to get to there. She decided to forget that dream and move on to Plan B, whatever that might turn out to be. Driving to work, she bemoaned her situation to Paddy Flynn, an Irish journalist who was teaching at the college that semester. Paddy had read her light essays, had some idea of what she could do. "Go to Cuba," he had said. "It's hot news, but the press bureaus have pulled their people out. You'll place anything you write." That did it.

She made an appointment with the Cuban consul, who gave her the necessary information about documents and exit permits, a tiny cup of strong black coffee and a load of pamphlets.

Searching for topics, she read about the year of *alfabeticatión*, when everyone had learned to read, about immunization against polio. Amazing. She would make her name breaking all this to Canadian newspapers.

The morning she left, she was excited, but worried about her daughter.

"I'll be okay with Brenda. It's your turn." Earl told her. "This will be a good experience for us."

She fought the need to cling as he hugged her goodbye; tried to ignore the wrench of pain at leaving Brenda.

Her anticipation became a frenzy as she worked late at night in order to leave the house in manageable condition.

She reminded Earl. "Don't forget Brenda's dental appointment September 12th. Our winter clothes have to be picked up at the dry cleaners."

By the time she was aboard the plane, she was preoccupied with the task ahead. Whom to interview? Where to focus? Education, she thought. Or maybe health.

In Miami, she encountered suspicion and hostility from U.S. Immigration officials. "You a diplomat?" an officer asked.

"No."

"Then why are you going to Havana? Everyone else is trying to get out."

"I'm a journalist. I want to write about what's happening down there."

"It says there on your passport, occupation, professor. Got a press card?"

"I've an editor friend, he said he could help."

"Where are you staying? What hotel?"

"Havana Libre."

"You're asking for trouble." The officer strode off and gave her passport to another officer in a glassed-in cubicle. This officer stared at her, shrugged, stamped the passport and returned it to the first man. With a disapproving look, he gave it back to her and commanded, "Wait out there by Gate 3C."

His suspicious attitude made her feel as if she were smuggling or spying.

Hungry, she strode to a lunch counter and ordered coffee and a toasted bacon sandwich. She wolfed it down and gulped her coffee. She felt better until she handed the cashier a ten-dollar bill.

"What the hell's *that*?" the cashier demanded, slapping the bill back to her.

"Ten dollars."

"Canadian. Your funny money is no good here." Stools swiveled as diners turned to see what a Canadian looked like. Reluctant, Linda took a traveler's check from her purse. She hadn't wanted to change these until she got to Havana. The cashier took her time before commanding, "Sign." Linda obeyed and waited while the woman counted out U.S. bills.

She went to search for Gate 3C. When she found it, she saw a middle-aged couple seated on a bench. Good, she thought. I need someone to talk to. I'm defensive because of how I've been treated here.

The couple looked friendly. The plump, auburn-haired woman wore a blue print dress with a boat neck that exposed freckled white skin. The man was red-faced, perhaps because he wore a tightly knotted tie that made his neck bulge over his shirt collar. Linda glanced at their luggage tags. Same code as hers.

She sat opposite them and asked, "Are you going to Havana?"

"Yes."

"I'm so relieved. I was afraid I'd be traveling alone."

They stared. At her new olive green dress, her stockings, heels and white gloves.

"What brings you to Havana?" she asked.

"A mission posting," the woman announced.

Linda had intended to identify herself as a journalist but figured that "professor" would go over better with missionaries.

"I'm a professor. I'm curious about what's going on in Cuba."

The couple exchanged glances before each returned to reading a copy of something called *The Good News Bible*.

Feeling rebuffed and impatient, Linda jumped in, "I have my own mission. I'm bringing a serum to Havana. There's this little girl . . ."

"You fell for that?" The woman smiled. The two set their magazines down and chuckled.

"They tried that on us," the woman said, "but we'd been warned. Be careful. It could be drugs, anything." She picked up her book.

Now scared about the serum, Linda worried about what might happen in Cuba. She could be imprisoned or disappear and never see Brenda or Earl again.

Seeking comfort, she reached for her bag and took out Alejo Carpentier's *The Lost Steps*. She found it hard to imagine this novelist as Cuba's minister of culture. It was also hard to imagine Castro, a Jesuit-educated lawyer, as a dictator.

She flipped through pages until, after an announcement, the couple rose and picked up their magazines and luggage to board. A uniformed official slid open the gate and Linda followed the couple to a rickety turbo prop. As she ascended the steps a man rushed through the gate and called, "*Señora*! Did you get the medicine?"

"Yes."

"Thank God! My poor father needs that heart medicine to save his life."

Polio serum. Heart medicine.

What was she carrying? Those men could be counter-revolutionaries trying to blow up the plane.

She placed her purse containing passport, money and medicine on a seat in a row across the aisle and sat as far away from it as possible. She took a deep breath as the plane taxied along the runway and sat rigid with terror. The second leg of her first travel abroad ruined. She'd dreamed of thrills, never of danger.

From the plane window, José Marti Airport looked like an army base with its dull olive camouflage colors that merged into palm trees. Linda walked across the aisle and picked up her purse. When the steward opened the door, gusts of heat struck. Awed, she trailed behind the missionaries, pausing to look around. Everything was dull green, hot, unreal.

A group of soldiers marched towards the plane: with a twist of his shoulder, one pointed a gun, indicating the direction she was to follow. Surprised, she noticed that two of these soldiers were women wearing make-up. She followed and waited while the missionaries presented their documents. She mopped her forehead and brushed her hair off her face. One of the soldiers smiled and asked, "*Americana*?"

"No," she answered. "*Soy Canadiense.*"

"*Muy bien,*" he replied.

She was struggling to phrase a Spanish response when a cubicle door opened. The soldiers led the missionaries out another exit before escorting her into the room where she presented her passport and permit to the official. In careful Spanish she lied, "*Soy una amiga de la revolución,*" the way Elsie, a friend who had lived in Cuba had coached her to do.

"You'll be in the way," Elsie had warned, "but if you must go, learn some important Spanish. '*Soy una amiga de la revolución . . .*'"

"I'm not a friend of the revolution, Elsie. I'm going there to be objective."

"Sure," Elsie said. "Here's an address to use if you need help. It's a friend of mine, Martha Anderson. A teacher from Saskatchewan. She's fluent in Spanish and an official in the Ministry of Education. Knows all the important people."

Linda had retorted. "I can make it on my own."

Elsie continued. "Another thing. They sing *El International* after meetings. You'll probably attend some, so sing. Try to fit in."

Elsie had thrust Martha's card and the Spanish version of *The International* into her hand. "Keep these. You never know."

The officer stretched across the desk to shake her hand. Two more soldiers arrived with her suitcase, set it on a low table and opened it. On top, pamphlets from the consul, a Spanish dictionary. The official picked up her silk fuschia dress and said, "*Muy bonita. Muy bonita señorita.*" He dropped it, slammed the suitcase shut and pointed to her shoulder bag. Out came the Carpentier novel and Linda's improvised Spanish. "*El esta un autor muy bueno. El esta ministro do cultura. Verdad*?" There was murmuring between the official and the soldiers. As he reached for her purse, she took his hand and shook it.

"*Muchas gracias, señor.*"

The officer hesitated, shrugged and released her hand. "I hope you will enjoy Cuba. You may go now."

The soldiers led her out and summoned a taxi. Another soldier leapt across the road to a border of foliage, plucked a flower and, smiling, handed it to her.

She held the waxy jasmine blossom to her face and smiled at the soldier.

An ancient Chevy rattled up. Its driver took her luggage and held the door. She leaned against the battered upholstery in relief. So far, she thought, just a gorgeous flower and gallant men. No exploding purse.

As the driver started, she said, "*Havana Libre.*"

"*No, señorita. Vamos para Hotel Riviera.*"

She blurted in English. "I'm expected at Havana Libre! That's what I told officials." The man shrugged. She repeated, "*Havana Libre, por favor!*" As he drove along the Malecón, she enjoyed the ocean breeze. Eventually they arrived at a huge hotel. *Hotel Riviera*.

"*Señor, por favor, el hotel Havana Libre!*"

"*No, señorita,*" he said, "*Aqui. Vamonos.*"

"*Cuanto costa?*"

"*Nada.*"

He opened the car door, picked up her suitcase and led her through the entrance and up to the desk. She had been advised not to tip because Cubans disapproved. She shook his hand. "*Muchas gracias.*"

To her relief, the desk clerk spoke English. "Please, may I see your passport?"

"There's been a mistake. I plan to stay at the Havana Libre."

"You will enjoy it here. A change has been made." He pushed a pen and the form towards her.

She wanted to scream. Commie bigwigs, the people from whom she'd get information for her article, stayed at the Libre. Not here. The clerk read disapproval on her face.

"You are on the Malecón, our ocean drive. This is more luxurious for a visitor."

Linda took her passport from her purse and signed the register. The clerk summoned a tall man to carry her bags and said, "At your floor, police will examine your luggage."

"Thanks." She was sweating, her dress rumpled, but young men seated in the lounge smiled at her.

She was glad, now, to have the phone number of Martha Anderson, Elsie's friend. If the police found the fake serum, she'd need help to stay out of trouble. And she would demand a transfer to Havana Libre.

The elevator stopped at the ninth floor. The man led them towards her room where a policeman stood at the door.

"*Buenas tardes, Señora Campbell.*"

Now she was frightened. They knew her name and everything. The switch had been planned. To her imagination, a sign of heavy intelligence stuff.

The officer set her suitcase on the luggage rack, opened it and rummaged around, carefully avoiding tampons and lingerie. He asked, "How long are you staying?"

"*Seis semanas.*" When he reached for her shoulder bag, she said, "*Soy una amiga de la revolución!*" Then, holding up Carpentier's book, she said, "*El esta un autor muy bueno!*"

The policeman's face brightened, he asked, "You read him in Canada?"

"Of course."

"If you have problems, please report to the desk. We must keep you safe in our country." He nodded and left.

She wanted to shower but flopped down on the bed, clutching her jasmine. Now the scent was sickening. She was hungry, tired and scared, but must decide what to do about the contraband bottle. She thought of her brother the lawyer. "Obey the law of the land." The policeman was nice. So what if he was a Commie? A foreigner was not above the law of the land. She walked to the sink, splashed water on her face, strode to the elevator, descended and approached the desk clerk.

"May I help you?"

"Yes."

She relayed her story of the men at Miami airport, took the bottle from her purse and gave it to the clerk.

"There's a name and a phone number here. I'm tired and unsure of the correct procedure. Would you please take care of it?"

"Of course."

Now, Linda thought, I can shower, change and eat. Panic left as she returned to her room. Nearing her door, she heard the phone and rushed to pick up the receiver.

"*Buenas tardes.*"

"You are *Señora* Campbell from Toronto?" The voice was assertive, the English clear and unaccented.

"Yes."

"You have medicine for my child? My husband tele-phoned me about you. I phoned the Libre but you weren't there. I phoned all the big hotels until I found you. I'd like to meet you and show you around."

Linda knew she had done the right thing. If this woman's child was so sick, why the offer to "show you around"? She waited.

"Mrs Campbell?"

"I left the medicine at the desk for you."

The woman hung up.

Linda dialed the number that Elsie had given her and got a receptionist who answered with an exuberant, "*Venceremos*," but could not understand Linda as she repeated. "Martha Anderson, Martha Anderson." Finally a voice announced, "Martha Anderson."

"Hello, I'm Linda Campbell, from Toronto? A friend of Elsie's. She suggested that I call you if I had any problems."

"From Toronto? Where are you are staying? I'll be right over."

"I'm at Hotel Riviera. That's kind of you, but perhaps I could just explain . . ."

"Meet me in the lobby."

"How will you know me?"

Martha laughed. "Easy. See you soon."

Linda walked through the lobby and sat down on an or-nate stuffed chair, one of several chairs circling a glass coffee table. The desk clerk waved as she passed. Men of all ages lounged about. There were no women in sight. No wonder Martha knew Linda would recognize her. Feeling conspicuous, Linda walked to a newsstand, bought a copy of *Hoy* to hide behind and returned to her chair. Male eyes followed as she crossed the floor. She had caught the eye of a young man in khaki when a short, stocky young woman burst into the lobby and darted across to embrace her as she blurted, "It's so good to see someone from home! How's Elsie?"

"Great. Working hard. Causes. You know Elsie."

"Yes. Now, what was your problem, Linda?"

Martha wore a simple beige cotton dress and sandals. Tanned skin emphasized her bright blue eyes and sun-streaked blond hair. Linda trusted her at once and poured out her experience of the Miami men. The serum/heart medicine, the caller, and her thought about the "law of the land."

"You did *exactly* the right thing. It could have been drugs or an attempt to link you up with counter-revolutionaries. I was alarmed to hear of a Canadian woman coming here alone at this time. But you will have made a good impression reporting that incident. I'm not sure what your connection to Elsie is or why you came here."

"I met her at a Cuban film." To avoid further questions and get on with her work, Linda told Martha about her plan to write. She did not tell her that she was fed up with teaching. She didn't think it would go over well with someone committed enough to a foreign revolution to leave Canada. Like her friend Elsie, who had served in the militia and spoke about long stretches of food shortages and living on rice.

"I'm not sure what I want to write," Linda said. "The thrust in newspapers back home is of a possible attack on the U.S. by Russians, but I've been reading about health care, nursery schools and the alphabetization program. It's just so amazing that this year everyone is learning to read!

I want to get around as much as I can, talk to people and see what's going on."

Martha smiled. "Would you be up to hearing Fidel tonight? He's addressing delegates to an educational conference at the Chaplin Theater."

"Really? Castro?"

"Really." Martha scribbled on the back of a card and handed it to her. "Be ready around nine o'clock. I'll have a friend pick you up. Show the driver the card." Martha looked at her watch. She had become businesslike, but her face softened as she asked, "Are the leaves back home turning yet?"

"Just starting. I didn't think you'd remember things like that. Everything here is so beautiful."

"I miss the seasons. The crunch of the first snowfall, the autumn colors, the crisp air. And apples!"

Linda had expected a rhetoric-spouting bureaucrat, not a homesick Canadian. Martha said, "I'll call you again and we'll get together. Have you eaten? There's not much, but we have lots of avocados."

"I haven't had time to eat. I've been on the run ever since I got here. I want to explore. I've never seen tropical flowers. The hibiscus is incredible and the scent of jasmine knocks me out!"

"A typical tourist reaction, but I'm glad you like it here. You'll get enough information for several articles in a couple weeks. I advise you to do that and head home. It *is* a tense time." She led Linda to the window. "Look, there's the Malecón — that road stretching along the coast. Over there, a U.S. warship. Waiting. Over there," she pointed toward the opposite side, "a Russian battleship. Ten days ago the U.S. battleship shelled the coast further down. I'll give you any help I can. Don't go out around four in the afternoon. It's the rainy season. You'll get drenched."

"I won't go out around four, but about going back so soon, no. I wanted to, you know, enjoy the ambience . . ."

"This is not the time. If you want a vacation with ambience, try another island." Aware that she had sounded harsh, Martha added, "It's hard for an outsider to understand. Don't hang around unless you're prepared to join the militia."

Linda remembered Elsie. "*You'll only be in the way.*"

Martha smiled. "Have a nap, hear Fidel and get back to me tomorrow. I'll set up meetings for you. *La Federación de las Mujeres* — that's a women's group. And people from the Committee for the Defense of the Revolution — they're self-policing neighborhood groups. And our nursery schools. So many women are back at school, taking jobs for the first time. That's worth writing home about."

Martha's suggestions made Linda feel trusted. They embraced and Martha bolted out the door.

Linda returned to her room and hung up her shirtmaker dress. The fuschia silk was out. Women would dress simply in a post-revolutionary country. The silk dress would make her look too North American, too gringo.

Cuban music blared forth from the radio, incessant, intrusive.

She showered, wrapped herself in a towel, turned off the radio and lay down on the bed. An irritating hum came from the radio. She turned it on and off again but the hum persisted. She stretched out on her bed, threw off the towel and lay nude in the heat.

She dozed, tossed, awoke; dozed, tossed, awoke. No real sleep. Vignettes of the day's events flew through her mind: kissing Brenda goodbye, kissing Earl goodby;

the Miami episode; the near misses by Havana customs inspectors; the phone call. Disjointed episodes. She grew restless, overcome by heat. The sheet beneath her was soaked in sweat.

Sounds on the street muted and vanished. Then there was a sudden drumming sound outside as a heavy downpour filled her room with cool air. She relaxed until she heard street sounds again. Quicker, as if the city too was suddenly refreshed.

Restored, she marveled at her luck. She would hear Fidel Castro her first night in Havana. How about that! She saw herself telling people about it back home.

Elsie had been right about needing a friend in Havana. Maybe she was right about learning the words to *The International.* Linda got up and took out the typewritten sheet. *Agrupemos, todos*, We all join together. She said the words aloud, read the anthem again. Then distraught, tore up the sheet.

It's all right to cooperate with the law to fit in, she thought, but I have my limits.

She slid into fresh underwear, decided against stockings and for heels, put on her tired green dress. She needed make-up. Even the gunslinging female militia soldiers had worn eye shadow, mascara and lipstick. She put on her white gloves. Better stick with little formalities to create a good impression. She headed for the lobby.

It was crowded with young men, milling about and spilling into and out of the bar. She checked her watch. 8:30.

A tall man left the front desk and asked, "*Señorita*, may I offer you a drink?"

Linda was still wary, but she had seen this man speaking

with hotel staff so assumed he was safe. "I wouldn't dare. I haven't time. I'm being picked up outside at nine."

"I know. *Señorita* Anderson has arranged for you to hear Fidel. You're very lucky. Your car will be late. It does not take long to drink a daiquiri. I am Tomás, with the hotel. Your driver will wait."

"Are you sure I have time?"

"Very sure." He took her hand and led her into the bar. The khaki-clad young men in the bar ceased chattering as they entered.

"*Dos Papa Doblés!*" Tomás snapped.

"Oh, you've read Hemingway." she said.

"He lived outside Havana. I could arrange for you to visit his old home."

"That would be marvelous." A waiter placed two huge frosted daiquiris before them.

"*Salud!*"

"*Salud!*"

Linda sipped while the man downed his drink. When she glanced at her watch, Tomás said, "You've lots of time."

Suspicious again, she decided that he had been sent to make sure she did not hear Fidel. How come he knew all about her meeting Martha, her evening plans? When she opened her purse, Tomás guessed her intent and put his hand over hers. "You are our guest, *Señorita*. I am the hotel coordinator, employed to ensure hospitality to our guests. This is your welcome drink."

"Thank you. You're very kind, but I'm worried that I'll miss hearing Castro."

"Fidel will not arrive until around ten o'clock. He will speak for three hours, maybe four."

"Won't people get bored?"

"Those invited are honored and would be insulted by a short speech."

Linda finished her drink. "That dacquiri was wonderful."

"Of course. Our best white rum, fresh limes. If I see you after you return tonight, I'll order another for you."

As he escorted her outside, she was aware of smiles and whispers from men in the bar.

"Who are all those guys?"

"Students. From Columbia, Mexico, Venezuela, Chile. They have come here to help build and protect a new Cuba. They serve in the army, but meanwhile attend school. A few of the older men are Russian, or from the Eastern bloc, *técnicos*."

"Why are they smiling? What's so funny?"

"One, you are the only woman here. Two, forgive me, *Señorita*. Nobody wears gloves in the tropics."

At the entrance he said, "I've guests to attend to. A French photographer is arriving tonight. Please excuse me."

Outside, in the hotel garden, Linda thrust her gloves into her purse and leaned against a wall. A green lizard darted out from foliage. The lizards were loathsome but the flowers were beautiful.

She looked at her watch. It was 9:15 and still no car. Had the plan been hoax? She was too hungry and tired to decide what to do. Take a taxi? Phone Martha?

A Jeep arrived and a tall man in army fatigues called out, "*Señorita* Campbell?"

As she ran to the Jeep, he leapt out to open the door and let her in beside him.

"I'm a friend of Martha's, Federico Cruz."

Lucky Martha, Linda thought. No wonder she stays.

Linda reminds herself. I am married.

Estoy casada.

"I'm driving you to hear Fidel." He switched to Spanish. "*Esta casada?*"

"No," she said, "I just had a nap." The man looked confused.

She remembered giggles in her Spanish conversation class, the confusion between "*cansar*" to be tired, and "*casar*" to be married.

In answer to, "Are you married?" she had replied, "I just had a nap."

"Something is funny? No?"

"No, I'm just tired," she said, and wondered if her mistake had been deliberate. An unconscious slip to avoid the truth.

"Martha says you are a friend of Elsie?"

"Yes."

"Do you also belong to the same sympathetic groups as Elsie?"

"In a way."

Linda considered Martha's suggestion that she go home early. A U.S. warship really *had* shelled the coast. There really were Russians here. And despite Elsie, Martha and the handsome guy in uniform beside her, she did *not* feel that she was one of them. She was a left-wing dropout. Militarism was scary, the advance knowledge about her was an indication of an effective intelligence system.

Nevertheless, she was thrilled to be here. Her first foreign country was beautiful. The air was heavy with scent. Of jasmine and drama. Flowers and guns. Lizards.

"It's a gorgeous country!" she gushed.

"The tropics are seductive. Especially Havana, the most sensual city in the world. Are you comfortable?

Do you have any problems?"

"A minor thing. I can't turn off my radio."

"I thought Elsie would have told you. Hotels are bugged. It's done through radios."

"Bugged? I thought that only happened in spy stories."

"Our country is in crisis. Even Martha's activities are monitored. She's a foreigner, no matter what her loyalty to Cuba."

He parked the Jeep. Crowds milled outside the Chaplin Theater. As they parted to make way for Federico, she realized he must be important. He kept his hand on her shoulder as he ushered her to the entrance, spoke to an official at door and said, "Someone will drive you back. Perhaps myself. Wait here after the speech. Right here."

"Thank you."

Seated alone in a row marked *El Cuerpo Diplomático do Canada* she wonders who will sit in the empty seats. Canada has maintained its embassy here, so perhaps she will meet other Canadians. She looks at her watch: 9:50, 10:15. At 10:45, the guards stand aside to let a crowd rush in and fill vacant seats. A group of women holding toddlers and babies fill a row marked *Los Estados Unidos*. Other Cubans smile and join her to become instant diplomats of Canada.

There is a sound of rustling as the crowd rises to its feet chanting. "*Fidel! Fidel! Fidel!*" This mass response frightens her. She wants to leave, head back to the hotel, home to Canada. There are sounds on the stage; rustling in front. Armed militiamen appear.

Fidel Castro enters and stands on the stage less than seven feet away from her. The crowd bursts into another uproar. He holds up his hand and smiles. Like a priest, she thinks. There is silence, then a tinny loudspeaker plays the Cuban national anthem. The crowd rise and join hands, swaying as they sing.

Linda shakes her head, refusing to link hands. At the anthem's conclusion, the audience sits. A woman introduces the minister of education, who in turn introduces Fidel. Chanting resumes. The audience is silenced by the raised priestly hand.

The auditorium is not air conditioned. Sweat glues Linda's dress to her back, which makes her doubly aware of how cool and immaculate Castro is. His trousers and shirt are crisp. She had expected sweaty, sloppy, as pictured in American newspaper cartoons. His voice, like music, builds to a crescendo, softens to a diminuendo. She has caught his use of repetitive parallel construction. The throng is rapt as he explains how many people have learned to read, how many children have started school. Linda yields to his voice, the rhythm of his speech. A sensation like fighting a current in a swift river and being pulled in. At intervals, Fidel pauses, strides offstage to take a drink from an attendant. Before speaking again, he makes eye contact with the audience. When he turns, Linda sees back muscles move under his shirt. His crisp *dry* shirt. There is control in his voice, his walk, his gestures. This is charisma.

Much later, his voice grows quiet. The pitch rises when he concludes, "*Venceremos! Vive el año do alphabetizatión! Vive la revolución! Vive Cuba libre!*"

The crowd chants, "*Vive Cuba libre!*" When the loudspeaker plays *El International*, girls distribute jasmine blossoms to the audience. Linda rises with the others.

She lifts her blossom and breathes its heavy scent. She feels trapped, wants to flee. Everyone is reaching out to hold the jasmine-clutching hand of a neighbor, making a floral chain. She becomes a link and tears fall as a familiar voice sings *El International* with the swaying throng.

It is her own voice.

Tourist

January, 2003

Linda strides along the shore. Hearing the surf, she remembers sounds of Cuba long ago. When she arrived, palms swished Russian consonants; when she left, palms keened in the wind.

Last night, New Year's Eve, she was lulled to sleep by Cuban music as departing tourists danced out the old year. This morning, she woke up and heard laughing voices as a new tour group arrived. She wonders what this group will be like. Single or married? Young or old?

Old? I'm not old, she thinks, I've just had too many endings lately.

Her daughter was launched, her own marriage was long over and she had just retired from teaching. Fighting a sense of loss, she traveled to Cuba, her favorite destination.

On her walk, she passes the same smiling barefoot woman she passes every morning and they exchange their usual *"Buenos días."* This encounter always upsets Linda because she knows that the woman's smile is a plea for clothing and cosmetics.

Cuba was not supposed to turn out like this.

She strolls into the dining room where she likes to sit alone drinking strong black coffee. She halts, surprised to see a young woman sitting and smoking at the table she has claimed as her own. The girl is barefoot and wears a blue tank top and jeans; blonde hair sweeps over her hunched shoulders. Linda does not want company and hates smokers but knows that she must welcome this newcomer. The staff would think her snobbish, avoiding her *compañera*. She also knows that although her political background gives her an edge here, Cubans would not excuse unfriendliness. Besides, she wonders. What's this girl seeking?

They're all seeking something, these rootless tourists. Over the years, Linda has watched them arrive and down free drinks; watched their greedy Northern hustle for cheap rum, good cigars and Latin romance.

She accepts her fate and sits down opposite the young woman.

"Hi. I'm Linda Campbell. May I join you?"

"Yes. *Please!* I'm Megan Sutherland."

"Did you celebrate last night, Megan?"

"I can't drink. I'm on Prozac. It hasn't kicked in yet." She puts down her cigarette, drops her head in her hands and sobs.

Here I go again, Linda thinks. Collecting needy people. What else is there for me? Romance?

In the summer of 1962, Linda had not been looking for romance. She needed a change, a break from her husband's expectations. Clean socks, gourmet meals, starched shirts. She wanted to fly away like he did. Always leaving to travel in search of minerals in exotic places. Africa, Indonesia.

She *had* loved Earl. They met as students in the 50s and were considered an ideal couple who did the expected things. Got engaged, married; bought a house, had a baby. Linda's return to teaching had been unexpected. With Earl away so much, she had craved an outside interest.

That summer, she had hoped to leave teaching and become a journalist. Realizing that she had never flown, she searched for exciting travel destinations and chose Cuba. Warnings from Elsie Scott, an old school friend, a Canadian who had served in Cuba's militia, only whetted her need for adventure. Brenda was starting play school and Earl approved. Why not?

Linda had arrived in Havana frightened by the hostile remarks of U.S. officials in Miami. Frightened, but intrigued. Adventure, foreign language, foreign charm. When she checked in to Hotel Riviera, Tomás, a hotel representative greeted her. "Welcome to Cuba! After you settle in your room, meet me here for a drink."

She had agreed. Registering, she felt men's eyes on her and hurried out of the lobby. She bathed, changed and explored the hotel before meeting Tomás.

He had taken her hand and led her to the bar where he ordered *mojitos*. Or were they *dacquiris?* One of those. Linda remembers sipping her drink and feeling like a Hemingway heroine.

She had asked Tomás about the khaki-clad men in the lobby.

"They're from Central and South America and Algeria," he said. "Here to study and build the new Cuba. If needed, to serve in the army. They're good men. Busy training, but if you need help, ask one of them or leave me a message." Later, he led her to the lobby and excused himself.

It had been an amazing time. On that first night in Havana, she had heard Fidel Castro speak. After she returned to the hotel, she looked for Tomás, needing to talk. As she searched for him, a young man approached. "I am Rafael Sanchez. May I join you? I wish to practice English."

"I'm Linda Campbell. Thanks, I could use a walk. I need to calm down."

"Of course." The young man had led her out to the *Malecón*. He was slight, dark, and looked not much older than her college students. As they strolled, she poured out an account of her trip from Toronto and of hearing Fidel. When she was finally talked out, Rafael told her he was studying to be a doctor. In a garden, he picked a jasmine blossom and placed it behind her ear. At the elevator, he invited her to swim the next afternoon.

Every day after that, they would walk, swim and talk. When he learned that she admired Hemingway, he had taken her to see a gorgeous old pink building, the Havana hotel where Papa Hemingway had stayed.

One morning, she set out alone to explore Old Havana. Captivated by the architecture of the old buildings and blazing, heavy-scented gardens, she became dazed in the heat and lost her way. She leaned on a bridge rail that meandered through jungles of vines. To her relief, Daniel, an Algerian, found her and led her back to the hotel.

She swam with Daniel but rejected his other invitations. There were so many lonely men here and so few women.

She had decided to phone home. She needed to hear Brenda, talk to Earl. After many tries, her call could not get through.

Linda watches the staff assemble platters of grapefruit, oranges and bananas. Sonya, the cook, is making breakfast. Linda feels guilty. She knows that Cubans don't eat as well as tourists, but she would feel guiltier if she didn't eat well and hurt their pride. She hopes that all Megan needs is a good meal. "Let's have breakfast," she says. "It's the best meal here."

Tears stream down Megan's cheeks. "I'm not hungry. You go ahead."

"Okay. Excuse me." Linda rushes to the counter, grabs a tray and greets Sonya, presiding over eggs, pancakes and syrup made from leftover fruit and rinds. She takes an egg, a pancake, a banana, then rushes to the coffee urn. It will be bitter but strong, left over from last night's party.

Sonya follows her, smiling. "Do you have enough, Linda?"

"*Si. Tengo mucho!*"

Linda returns to see Megan clutching a cigarette and exhaling clouds of smoke.

She waves her cigarette. "I hope you don't mind. I just had to."

"It's okay."

"It's not okay . . . I do everything not okay . . . my boyfriend and I broke up . . . I tried to do the right things . . . got sick . . . the doctor gave me Prozac . . . it's not working . . . he said a couple of weeks before it kicks in."

Linda cuts her pancake into little squares. "That's a lot to deal with," she says. "What about your boyfriend?"

"Gone back to Argentina . . . he's the oldest . . . his family."

Family, yes. That first visit. In September, Tomás and Martha had taken her aside and told her to leave unless she was prepared to remain indefinitely. Unable to face separation from Brenda, she had left weeping. After her return to Toronto, the Missile Crisis. She had been too upset to even think of writing. How could she be objective?

Newscasts. Brenda clutching her skirt. Where was Earl? Australia? Indonesia?

Linda finishes her pancake and egg. "It's great, Megan. You should eat."

Megan butts her cigarette. "I'll try." She saunters to the buffet and returns with the grapefruit. She eats it and darts back to the buffet to load her tray with pancakes, eggs and sausages.

Relieved to see her eat, Linda wonders if Megan had only been suffering jet lag or PMS.

She lights another cigarette. "I'm sorry, Linda. Depressives are *boring*. I hate being a bore."

"It's okay. Never apologize to me about depression. I wrote the book."

"You? Depressed?"

"Yes, most of my life. Like being diabetic. You learn what to do, what to avoid."

"But that's *so* funny!"

"Funny goes with the territory. The flip side."

"And stuff to avoid? You mean men? Foreign men?"

"Right. Spaniards, Lithuanians, endorphins."

When Megan giggles, Linda is reminded that her daughter is humorless. Brenda works with computers and is married to a broker. Maybe she should contact Brenda after she gets back to Toronto. She hasn't seen her since shortly after her daughter went to Sulawesi to Earl's wedding. She and her daughter have nothing in common.

Now Linda wonders. What if I hadn't gone back to Havana after the crisis, during the embargo, only to learn that Rafael had married?

After that second trip she had to go through Mexico to get home. The CIA had photographed her at the airport. Word reached Earl's company, his job was on the line.

When he questioned her, she told him about Rafael. "Never mind your little tourist affair," he had said, "All that matters is my work!"

She stayed with him for another year, but the marriage died with that sentence.

Other tourists straggle down to breakfast. Honeymooners, singles, pensioners. Linda scans their bland Canadian faces and decides to stay with Megan.

"Let's go biking, Megan. We can rent bikes at the bar."

"I'm going scuba diving."

"You scuba dive? I'm impressed."

"Not me. My friend Ally. She's so talented! I'm going along for the ride. It depends on weather and tides. We teach at the same college."

"What do you teach?"

"Calculus."

"I loathed math. I taught English. What about Ally?"

"Sharp. Women's studies. It was her idea to come here. Spanish immersion. To cure me." Her lips quiver. She clutches her arms around her waist, rocking.

Linda changes the subject. "The Argentinian? What was his name?"

"Pablo. Manual laborer. So warm, so tender. I look around, should think, Wow, Cuba. Wow, Castro. No. Just, like, why am I here?"

"When did you break up with Pablo?"

"Three years ago."

"That's a long time to grieve alone."

"Not *alone*. There was Mario. Salvadorean. Rebound. The Spanish thing."

"There's a lovely word, Megan, for 'the Spanish thing.' *Duende*."

"*Du-en-de*," she mouths. Her face lights up. "*Duende?*"

"Yes. Poets use it. Lorca. Dark grief, angst, mischief. Untranslatable."

"*Du-en-de, du-en-de, du-en-de*." Megan mouths the word.

A short, dark woman bounds up and asks Megan, "Are you okay?"

"Really okay! Ally, meet Linda, my new friend. Better than my shrink."

Ally grasps Linda's hand. "Great to meet you."

"I'm happy to meet *you*. I'm impressed by your concern for your colleague."

"Megan overestimates me, Linda."

Linda notes her easy smile. A go-getter, a networker.

"Megan," Ally says, "You're off the hook for the dive. The weather is bad but the guide will take me fishing now that you're in good hands. See you, Linda," she spins around on her broad bare feet and shouts, "Ain't life a trip!"

"This is great," Megan says. "I hate holding Ally back. I'm just not into active stuff. I'm better here with you. I can tell you anything."

I hope not, Linda thinks, but says, "What are your hobbies? What do you read?"

"Reading makes me sad."

"We could go into Havana. It's a gorgeous city. The architecture is magnificent."

"I don't feel like going too far away from the resort."

"Have you any other interests?"

"I paint. My sketch pad and pencils are here in my pack."

"Great! Let's go outside and see what you can do."

Linda leads her to the palm-ringed terrace, sprawls on a chaise and points to a chair and table. "There, Megan. Your very own studio."

Megan shakes her head and crouches on the floor beside her.

Linda asks, "What artists do you like? Any favorites?"

"I don't *follow* art. I'm not a follower." Megan grabs her pack, takes out a pad and a stub of charcoal. "What should I sketch?"

"Whatever pops into your mind."

Megan does not stall. She makes rapid strokes, views her work, continues.

Linda wonders what Megan will produce. A bowl of fruit? A vase of flowers? At college exhibits, she recalls, there had always been bowls of fruit, vases of flowers.

Seeing Megan absorbed, Linda rises to sneak away for a book.

Megan whimpers, "You're running away?"

"I'm going to get a book."

"You'll come back? Promise?"

"I'll be back."

"Okay."

Linda intends to stall as long as possible.

In her room, she picks up a paperback and suntan lotion and sees that her freshly made bed has been decorated with towels shaped into swans. The maid has left a printed note on her pillow.

DEAR LINDA I HOPE YOU LIKE ROOM.
I LIKE TO PRACTICE ENGLISH.

She is touched by the note, the effort to please. Now she will leave a generous tip. Times have changed in Socialist Cuba.

She locks her door and heads to the bar. A mistake.

The bartender introduces another of the Cubans who visit resorts in search of a contact in Canada.

Today's visitor is a school principal with a Ph.D. As he offers his tattered business card, Linda hates accepting it — doing so sets up hope — but she is impressed by the young man's careful English.

She orders them both rum and coke and asks, "Where did you learn English?"

"From my father. He's a doctor. He learned from tourists."

She looks at his card.

Alfredo Sanchez
Doctor en Pedagogía
Universidad de la Habana

It's a common name, she thinks, a coincidence, but asks, "Has your father ever visited Canada?"

"No, but he has friends there from before the Crisis."

"What about your family? Do you have brothers and sisters?"

"A sister. She lived with our mother after our parents divorced."

How to meet his father? Ah, Megan!

"I've met a depressed young woman. Could your father come and see her? We'd pay in U.S. dollars, I know they're needed here."

"We could visit him nearby where he cares for patients in an old people's home. You must not pay, but if you have aspirins, vitamins, soap to donate, he'd be grateful."

"Done. When may we go?"

"Tomorrow? Could you cycle?"

"Of course."

"My father lives with his patients and he, too, gets depressed. He can't do much for them. They're old and dying. It's hard, knowing his patients will die."

It's hard for us all to know we'll die, she thinks, but says, "Come and meet my friend."

He shrugs. "Okay."

Yes, that shrug is Rafael's gesture. She must know about him. A new wife? A girlfriend? What about Alfredo himself? Yes, safer.

As she leads him to the terrace, she asks, "Are you married, Alfredo? Children?"

"A son. I miss him — my wife remarried. A Canadian. My son could live with me if I get to Canada."

Megan is absorbed in sketching as they approach.

"Megan, here's someone to meet you, Alfredo Sanchez. He's a teacher and wants work in Canada."

Megan sees Alfredo. She flings back her hair, sets down charcoal and pad to offer her hand. "Hi Alfredo. What do you teach?"

"Pedagogy. I teach teachers to teach."

"Fascinating!"

He asks, "May I see your sketches?"

"No," Megan says. "I was just killing time until Linda came back."

"Alfredo's father is a doctor," Linda says. "If you need to talk to someone, he might help you."

"I'm better. The medication must be working. Alfredo, please sit down."

"Sorry, no time today, but tomorrow Linda and I are cycling to the hospital with supplies. Would you like to come?"

"Great! I need exercise."

Linda smirks. Such enthusiasm after her refusal that morning.

"When should we be ready?" Megan asks.

"After breakfast before it's too hot."

"I'll look forward to it."

Linda says, "See you tomorrow."

When Megan offers her hand, Alfredo holds it and touches her shoulder.

Watching him leave, Megan blurts, "What a wonderful man! Tactile."

"Latin. You know about that."

"He has soulful eyes! Did you notice his eyes?"

"I did. Now, show me what you've done."

Megan passes her sketch to Linda, pats the chair and commands, "Sit there."

Relieved by Megan's mood change, Linda views the sketch and frowns. "Who is this? The Argentinian? The Guatemalan?"

"Wittgenstein. I saw his photograph in a philosophy text and liked his face."

Linda is confused. This airhead sketched Wittgenstein from memory? Wondering about Rafael, she had lost interest in Megan, but the sketch intrigues her. Wittgenstein?

"This is very good. Keep at it. I'll collect supplies. Think about what you need to discuss with Alfredo's father."

Megan asks, "Wouldn't a friend be just as good? Like Alfredo? What do you think?"

"I think you've a crush on him. If you want him for a friend, he can't be your shrink."

"Okay. I'll talk to his father. Let's get those supplies."

Linda follows her into the dining room. After receiving promises of donations for the hospital, the two eat lunch and sunbathe by the ocean. At dinner, Megan does not smoke.

Later, Linda showers, sets her hair and chooses a pink linen dress for the visit; goes to bed but cannot sleep.

At breakfast, Megan, in jeans and shirt, exclaims, "What a nifty dress for a bike ride!"

"If we're visiting the sick, we should look our best."

"You're so thoughtful, Linda." Megan digs into sausages and eggs and asks, "Aren't you eating?"

"No, all I need is coffee."

"Ally envies our trip. She went dancing last night. I'm going tonight."

So much for depression, Linda thinks.

After breakfast, they go to the bar for their bikes.

"My two best bicycles," the bartender says. "Ladies' bicycles from China."

Linda says, "We'll take good care of them."

Megan shrugs into her backpack.

Linda places her parcel in the carrier and feels dated.

Alfredo rounds the corner. "Good morning!" he calls. "Ready?"

"Yes," Megan replies.

"I'll lead," he says. "It's a rough road. Repairing roads is the least of our worries."

Megan pushes her bike up beside his.

Linda follows. Though relieved to have a weeping Megan off her back, she resents losing control. She pants biking uphill, while Megan speeds ahead.

Several miles later, Alfredo calls, "We're halfway there, Linda. Would you like to rest?"

"I'm fine."

When she catches up, Alfredo says, "We're near a hospital for Chernobyl orphans. Few other countries would take them."

Linda knows that she could not stand seeing those poor bald victims. She waits.

When neither Megan nor Linda offers to visit, Alfredo gets back on his bike.

Trailing, Linda sees herself at Rafael's side; imagines people impressed by her devotion.

"It's not much further," Alfredo calls. "See the hospital? We turn at the hilltop."

Megan and Alfredo get off the bikes.

Alfredo opens a rickety gate leading into a fenced area. Linda gets off her bike and gives him her bag.

"Thanks."

Megan passes him her pack. "Here's some coffee and canned stuff from the tourist shop."

"Thank you. That's wonderful."

Linda frowns.

"Look, Linda," Alfredo says. "There's our hospital."

She sees a once-luxurious building, perhaps the country estate of some pre-revolution landowner. It is old and rundown, surrounded by untrimmed tropical flowering bushes, their scent heady, exotic. Linda remembers that scent. Jasmine.

She pushes her bike closer and tells herself this visit is not about Rafael. It's about Cuba, about helping the hospital.

Patients sprawled on the veranda make their way down the steps and call, "Alfredo!"

Linda mops her forehead. She sees Alfredo smile at her and looks down. *He knows.*

The patients embrace Alfredo. He puts his arm around an old lady and greets the others, "Lucia! Carlos! Manuel!"

Megan not only accepts a hug from old Carlos, but returns it. Manuel, not to be outdone, kisses Linda's cheek. She is repelled by his breath, his body smell. That smell of sickness. Of age. A man stands on the verandah. He wears a frayed white shirt, jeans and running shoes. His hair is gray, his forehead lined.

Linda is shocked. This is not the Rafael she remembers, so young and immaculate in uniform.

He strides toward her, smiling. "We have met before, I think. Am I right?

"Yes," she says. "Long ago."

As Rafael leads Linda inside, Alfredo introduces Megan to the patients.

"You look well, Linda," Rafael says. "I think about you and remember that time."

"So do I. Walking and swimming, dreaming of great things to come. It didn't work, did it?"

"It worked for a while. Cuba has good health care and education. It's shortages that create problems."

"I want to help."

"I knew you'd come back."

"I've been back often. Because you were married, I kept away from Havana."

"I didn't mean come back to me. I meant to Cuba."

Oh, she thinks. That.

"You must meet my patients." He leads her to a ward filled with metal cots covered with worn mattresses, bare of sheets. Patients struggle onto their elbows and smile.

Linda wants to cringe from heat, hospital smells, sickness. This is not turning out how she imagined.

A patient calls Rafael, apparently curious about Linda. He explains, *"Canadiense. Muchos años pasados."*

When he comes back, she plays the role of concerned tourist. "Did the embargo affect your work?"

"Forget that." He leads her out of the ward and embraces her. She feels a sexual pull, as if her body remembers.

"Rafael, what are we doing?"

He opens a door. "My room."

It is bleak. A cot, a chair, a desk. A portrait of Fidel stares down from one wall, Ché from another. Once, yearning made her oblivious to surroundings. Now they matter.

"Will you stay?" he asks.

"In Cuba?"

"With me."

She stares at the walls. "There are problems."

"We could work things out. I've missed you."

She tries to pull away. "What about Alfredo and Megan?"

"They're busy." He leads her to the cot.

"*No!* We must join the others," she says. "*Now.*"

He strokes her cheek, "You've been corrupted."

"I haven't. I want to know the best thing to do. For the hospital."

"Of course. For the hospital." He changes from lover to guide. "We lack drugs. Vitamins. Soap. Bed sheets. Staff."

This is what Linda had thought she wanted. A romantic companion, meaning in life. She looks at Rafael and sees a tired face and gray hair. Sees fragility, age.

"I hoped it could happen," he says. "That you'd come back."

Linda says, "What about my daughter?"

"She's adult! Your living here shouldn't be a problem."

"I'll decide how to help. Here, or home raising money and collecting supplies."

"Why not work here and still keep in touch with your daughter and friends?"

"I need to know more. Where would I live?"

"With me, of course. And the others. Come and meet them."

Linda senses that he thinks she is considering the move and goes along with it. "Okay."

"You'll like my assistant." He leads her out and into a crowded ward. The walls are gray, the paint is peeling. Linda wonders how patients bear it, why he stays. He could move to Canada, but she knows that Cubans of his generation will tough out anything to make the dreams they fought for come true.

He speaks of drugs, patient numbers; answers her questions. She does not listen.

When they enter a ward, he calls, "Marcella! Come, meet Linda, my Canadian friend."

A short, pretty woman strides over. Linda scrutinizes her. Fifty? She wears a blue smock and sandals. Dark curls are pulled back by a scarf. "Hi," she hugs Linda.

Linda thinks, this woman is more than a nurse. No wonder he never tried to reach me. He wants supplies, a worker. If I stayed, where would that put Marcella? I must be fifteen years older than she is, but I'm better looking.

"Tell me about your work. Rafael is coaxing me to stay but I'm not a nurse. What am I getting into?" *There!*

"Wonderful! You'd relieve me of routine tasks to free me for nursing. Now, I take care of patients, do office work as well as keep records."

Linda comments, "You speak English very well."

"A Canadian volunteer taught me. A medical student from Winnipeg. A funny name. Win-ni-peg! He helped

one summer, but returned to Canada. He's in Africa now
with Doctors Without Borders."

Rafael smiles at their talk, at their apparent friendliness.

Linda wonders about the Canadian. Rafael is no competition for a husky prairie type.

"Could you show me around, Marcella?"

"Rafael will do that."

"It's been a pleasure meeting you. I'm sure we'll see
each other again."

"I hope so."

Linda takes Rafael's arm. "Come. The grand tour." She
bluffs as Rafael shows her around and explains what she
would do. Type, feed and bathe patients.

She looks at her watch. Four o'clock.

"It's time to go back. Will you join us for dinner?"

"Dinner is tempting, but I can't ride a bicycle. I was
injured in Angola. We're too short of gas for me to drive."

"Don't you get lonely? Don't you miss Havana?"

"No. I only go there to meet with officials or see my
daughter. Alfredo comes here. My patients and staff are
my family. If you stayed, we'd have each other."

Rafael waits. As Linda wonders what to say, Alfredo
and Megan appear.

Alfredo says, "Come and say goodbye. The patients
want to thank you for your visit."

Linda says. "I didn't visit. Your father has been showing
me around."

Megan exclaims. "The patients are sweet! I want to
come back."

Alfredo looks at his father. Rafael says, "I'm trying to
persuade Linda to stay."

Alfredo asks Linda, "What did you decide?"

"Nothing yet. It's a big step."

"Why not?" Megan asks. "You're free! I'd come if I could get out of my contract. Nobody asked me!"

"You would?" Alfredo asks. "The patients like you."

Linda wonders how long Megan would stay. Until the next lover?

She feels smug when Rafael says, "Megan, it would be complicated."

"What about our other plan, Megan?" Alfredo says. "A job for me at your college?"

"I'll work on that when I get home."

"Come," Rafael says, "The patients are waiting."

They follow him into a large, sparsely furnished room. Old men play dominoes; women sew scraps of cloth. They chatter, excited. When they are silent, Linda knows a speech is coming. In Cuba, any event is a big deal if there's a speech. Looking around, she realizes that many of these people are her own age.

Alfredo introduces Hugo, a tall frail man who speaks proudly, loud, like a political speech. The style admired here. Fidel's style. The guests sense that he is speaking about them.

Next, Alfredo introduces Elena, who holds up two rag dolls. Alfredo tells the visitors that these are made from scraps of cloth and given to patients for birthday presents. The patients are giving them their birthday dolls to thank them for bringing supplies.

As the visitors make the rounds, Megan embraces Elena and reaches out to other patients. Alfredo says, "This has been wonderful. Now it's time to go."

The patients cling to the visitors. When Rafael speaks, they back away to linger on the verandah.

Megan is teary. Alfredo's arm is around her. Linda watches them and realizes that the visit has been a good experience for everybody. For everybody else.

Megan clutches her doll. "This is sweet, when they have so little."

"They have spirit," Rafael says. "We care for each other here. I hope you both consider returning."

Miffed at the word "both," Linda turns to Rafael and says, "I'll help from home."

"And us?" he asks.

She hesitates.

He says, "I see."

Groups of chattering tourists wait in the airport. At Duty Free, Linda buys rum and coffee. Ally snags a bottle of single malt. Megan hugs her doll, watching the entrance until Alfredo dashes in and embraces her.

Ally nudges Linda and whispers, "See? No depression!" Linda wonders for how long. Megan has promised either to find Alfredo a job in Canada or to return to the hospital. She has visited the hospital daily and come back to the resort raving about Rafael, Marcella, the patients. She even visited the Chernobyl victims against Linda's advice and returned weeping. The next day she had maxed out her credit card on gifts and treats from the hotel tourist store to take back to the patients there.

Linda is eager to board the plane. The days have dragged. Megan was besotted with love; Ally preoccupied with athletic pursuits. Linda read whodunits and worked on a speech she would give when she got back to Canada. She will bring her rag doll and tell her colleagues all about the hospital. Brenda might be interested. Would it be worth the effort, trying to reconnect? No, she decides, we've gone too far on our separate ways.

Linda boards the plane. Fastening her seat belt, she thinks, I need something different. My own roots are Irish. I'll visit Ireland and explore ancient ruins. Everybody says it's a magical country.

As she presses against the window for a farewell look at Cuba, she sees clusters of palm trees swaying and leaning into each other. She cannot hear their sounds as jet noise signals takeoff.

There are palms growing in Ireland, she has read, cast adrift from southern countries long ago, still flourishing there today.

Costa Rica: The Snake Ranch

Erik

Celia

Zoe

Mimi

Erik

I've had it with these cheap sons of bitches who claim to love poetry but never buy a book.

Kenneth Rexroth

Bollocks. The usual library crowd. Here to be amused, here to see the great writer in his proper British tweeds (never mind that I've only spent a total of two years in Britain), here to be able to boast that they've attended a reading. Toronto literary ladies and writer wannabes with their nods, nudges and smiles as they pretend to understand. At least this bunch look like a well-heeled sort that will buy a book to be autographed. Not that any of them will read it. They're only here to be on show, the bitches.

I bring my comments to a close, smile, collect my papers, and hope to get off the podium without having to answer inane questions. A hand goes up. Hell and damnation.

Shit. It's that leering woman in the front row, a bitch wearing a hat. I smile at Hat Lady and ask, "Do you have a question?" Charm them, Erik, charm them!

"Mr Bjorseth, do you use a computer to write or do you write in longhand?"

Same old, same old. Christ, is none of them bright enough to come up with an original question? I smile and reply, "Computer for criticism, longhand for poetry."

Hat Lady persists, "There was a Mexican writer at Harbourfront, that nice, really famous writer Mexican Carlos Fuentes? In an interview, he told the audience that he wrote in longhand, that using a computer was like making love wearing a condom."

There are titters. I admire her bloody nerve, but to hell with her and her hat. To hell with Fuentes, to hell with the whole damned lot of nice, really famous writers. I'll fix her.

"What are you leading up to, dear lady? Do you want to learn about the creative process or are you just curious about my sexual practices?"

The bitch blushes. There are mixed responses from the audience. Some frown at her, others stare daggers at me. Only an older woman at the back smiles. Bless her silly little heart.

At least our exchange halted the question period. Amid mixed responses, wannabes tote books to a library volunteer drafted to the task in return for a free book. Wannabes buy the book in order to tell their pals all about "that outrageous poet." They won't read my poetry — they don't give a damn about poetry — but will demand that I write on the flyleaf, "To Joanne" or "Best wishes to Sara." However, sales make the ordeal worth it, so I smile and sign, sign and smile, hoping to subsidize my stay at that Costa Rican art colony. The locals call the place *La finca de las serpientes*, "the snake ranch." Boa constrictors have been found there.

I'll take snakes over snow any day. The bloody Canadian winter with its wretched hockey games and white-faced people drinking and cheering on Saturday nights. Until I'd arrived here, I never knew how terribly I'd miss Africa and Africans. The warmth, natural beauty, light and space. Here, everything is too damned white, too damned cold and dark and cramped. I'd wanted to get involved in a civilized sport like soccer or cricket. But after one sight of white expanses, I fled on a tour of South America.

I'd hoped to mingle with Canadian intellectuals and had been disappointed — most of the writers making names for themselves belonged to what I call the Nursery School of Writing. Youngsters. Graduates of wretched creative writing courses. I'm certain that this disappointment was mutual. I'd be a wealthy man if I had a dollar for every time I'd been asked if I knew Nelson Mandela or Jan de Klerk. When I admitted that I did not, my questioners' disappointment was palpable. However, when I informed colleagues that Coetzee had been one of my professors, the looks of awe led me to flee before my listeners genuflected. Also amusing were comments on my name. "Bjorseth. That's Dutch." Disbelief followed when I corrected these experts on South Africa to inform them that it was Norwegian. Not that the provincial mentality here is any worse than censorship back home. Indeed, no. I was relieved to leave apartheid.

In Capetown, broke after divorcing Jennifer, I headed for what I thought was a romantic, snowy wasteland. Living with an actress, I never knew what was real and what was performance. Except for Jen's affairs. I escaped with our daughter Janine, who was almost ready to leave home anyway, to the icy dominion. I took one look at Toronto and headed to South America where I had a great time hiking and hitch-hiking. Janine stayed on in Toronto to attend naturopathic college. In the south, I learned Spanish and found warmth. Upon return to Canada, I settled into a Brampton apartment, wrote reviews and travel pieces for Toronto dailies and married Megan, my editor. How was I to know that she really preferred women? After Megan, Newfoundland looked pretty damned good. By then Janine was working at a holistic health center — whatever that is — and I'd established enough of a reputation to obtain a writer-in-residence position in St John's.

Not that this Newfoundland junket was typical of Canadian life. Newfies are the most literate citizens of the True North and warmer-natured than Ontario people. But I didn't know that until I got there. Big frog, small puddle, I'd thought. Ho ho. Joke on me. An island of writers and prize-winners, all warm and friendly. But dear God, the climate! The cold, wet, grey climate!

As I put on my coat to leave, the smiler, who has not bought a book, touches my arm and says, "I don't know which I enjoyed more — your poetry or your response to that questioner."

"Not too far out of line? I just couldn't take it."

"You did the right thing. Her question was out of line. What did she want? A date? Your phone number?"

"I don't know. I'm ready to give up on these damned readings."

"You mustn't. Your poetry is marvelous and you read well. I enjoyed every minute. I'll have The Tundra bookstore back home in Sudbury order your book. Would you read up there?"

"You're connected with The Tundra? How kind of you to take an interest. How about a coffee? A drink?"

"Coffee would be great."

I am, indeed, shameless. A post-reading hanger-on with connections. Her connection to The Tundra, John Hall's bookstore, is a spot of luck. Authors keen to do their bit for the North, themselves and book sales give readings up there. Where it's cold and snowbound, people read. Melanie, a literary whore, works at The Tundra. As have other ladies eager to write who catch John Hall's eye. He's made a career of "launching" lady writers.

I escort my new fan out of the library. "Starbucks?"

"Sure."

Eager to dodge the other book ladies, I lead her to my old Toyota and hope it starts. After several tries it does and we're back in business. "I'm finishing another book. Literary criticism. My publisher wants it next March. Does The Tundra launch that sort of thing?"

"Absolutely. I'm Celia Hall. John Hall is my husband. Say the word."

The force is with me. I'll butter her up, talk her up.

"I thought so. I sensed that you were in touch with the world of letters."

"Not really. That's John's department. I'm an artist."

"Amazing! An artist! In what medium?"

"For a while I worked with acrylics, watercolors. Now I'm into oil sticks because they're fun. Fast and messy. I like messes."

Dear God, she's up to her ears in a mess. Does she know about Melanie? As I recall from my brief dalliance, Mel is hotter and younger than John's usual game. Poor Celia. Does she know what's up? Even if the Halls have one of those supposedly open marriages. It's been my experience that open marriages never work. They close down or blow up.

"I'm impressed. Who's your dealer?" I know this is equivalent to asking a writer if he has an agent, but hope she'll let it pass. I want to know if she's a real artist or another hobby painter.

"Igor Goretz in Yorkville. He's been my dealer since the seventies. That's when I started to work seriously."

Goretz. A tad popular, but respectable. "Where did you study? Ontario College of Art?"

"Eventually. At U Vic I decided not to be a writer and switched to art. I've never looked back. Never. No regrets. Never."

Too good to be true. She was at U Vic. I'd wager that she's about the same age as Zoe Anderson. If they knew each other back then, before Zoe got famous enough that a South African expat would write her biography, I could be in luck. A little undergraduate dirt. "Yes, but you kept up your literary interests. You married a bookstore owner known for discovering talented writers."

"Coincidence. John and I met on a blind date. Can you believe it?"

I can. John's not blind now and he wasn't then. Celia is a looker. Fit, blonde. Chic in a black pant suit. A sense of herself, her style.

Coffee and conversation over, I suggest keeping in touch by e-mail and she agrees. I drive her out to her daughter's place in the Beaches and return to my studio in Parkdale. Dragging out the Vic annual I'm using for research, I look in the arts section. Eureka, there she is! Celia McLeod, the same year as Zoe!

On the drive to her daughter's I learned that among many things we had in common, Celia just can't take Canadian winters. The next day I forwarded her the colony website and suggested that she apply. Then I e-mailed Patrick and told him to admit this great Canadian artist. Patrick and I had an understanding from my stay at *la finca* two years ago. I'd observed his dalliances with lonely women colonists, the muse-and-love seekers, and agreed to scout out likely prospects in return for reduced fees. A gentleman's agreement.

Celia e-mails to thank me for suggesting *la finca*. To her surprise and delight, she's been accepted.

She would never drop Zoe's name to me, knowing so many writers at The Tundra, but the two must certainly have been friends and would be delighted to reconnect. More points for me. I'm hoping for a romance with Zoe. Her sexual appetite is legend. She probably feels she knows me after all that correspondence before she finally agreed to come to Costa Rica to be interviewed for my book. She stalled and stalled, and I might have given up had not my agent — and hers — been so hot for a book. Besides, I need this book, and so does she. From the look of things, Zoe really is at that impasse her agent is afraid of.

Virile as I am, I might not keep up with her. I'd better get that prescription filled even though that "be prepared" aspect makes me feel more like a boy scout than a lover.

The flight down was pleasant. Celia proved to be good company. She reads widely and knows all the literary gossip. All I gather, except that about Melanie. Suspicious, yes. When she asked my opinion of Mel's writing, I shrugged, wanting to avoid a dangerous area, although I'm sure that Melanie will leave her mark in Canadian letters. And divorce courts.

I kept to literary topics before telling Celia that I'd seen her photo in a Vic annual the same year as Zoe. She bit, and told me that they'd been pals. After she mentioned some of Zoe's big-name lovers, I headed to the washroom with my notebook to jot down names and dates. When I returned, Celia was reluctant to discuss Zoe any further and changed the subject. We'd have a whole month at *la finca*, a whole month in which to find out more. Literary nonfiction is the hot ticket now. A juicy book about Zoe could make my name and give me an "in" to a relationship with her.

When Celia and I arrived at Customs in San José, I learned that traveling with an artist should be avoided. What a hassle! Boxes and boxes, which, being a gentleman, I carried. If the sun hadn't felt so great, I'd have been thoroughly pissed.

It was comforting to learn that Celia and I both loathe darkness and hunger for light. A bond about weather. A bond she'll need when she finds out about Melanie. Wives always find out. Nothing like a woman in need. Whose husband owns a bookstore.

We took a cab to the colony. Although Patrick's response at meeting Celia was bland, his wife Margo gushed, "The famous artist from Canada!"

Tired from the flight, Celia shot me a look when Margo suggested introducing her to others at the colony.

"Celia and I have had a long day. May she take a rain check?" After winning that round, I helped Patrick carry her supplies and settle her into a hilltop chalet.

I was bloody tired and needed a nap to get back in form before introducing myself to Zoe. I was keen to meet her, but not until I was at my best, not until I had a strategy. I do hope this connection to her will get my work known. Getting known is impossible for poets, which is why I undertook a work of nonfiction. The draft is finished — the literary references, critique and analysis. All it needs is a long interview with Zoe. I'll call that chapter "Under the Volcano," a nod to Malcolm Lowry fans that implies intimacy between Zoe and me near Mount Poas in Costa Rica. God, how I loathe these bloody mountains! I miss

Table Mountain back home, I miss mountain-top flirtations and long illicit climbs. Half the fun, in my day, had been that climbs were illegal. They're less exciting now. I miss the taste of *naarrtjie* that no tangerine will match; the smell of smoke from barbecued roasts and steaks, cooked over a *braai*. A barrel half with a grill on top. So many bloody memories . . .

Back to work, to my book. Still to be done are references to Zoe's days at Vic, complete with quotes from "a former colleague." Perfect!

What a relief to settle into my chalet. I'd requested one at ground level after living in an upper one last time. Climbing to Celia's was hard on my knees, but a swim and walk will get the stiffness out.

In the pool I swim until all the kinks and tensions are gone. It's a time for dreaming, for enjoying light and heat, reflections of trees in water.

I seem to be the only one about, except for a teenaged girl. A new staff member, sizing up the visitors? No, a tourist is my guess. The inevitable camera. Never one to be afraid of cameras, I go back to the diving board and pause a moment while she shoots. I swim a few more lengths and return to stretch out before the sun goes down. It's pleasant. The quiet, the rustle of trees, the aroma from shrubs of oregano. I'll pick some oregano to enhance salads and chops. Nothing lures a woman like an elegant meal cooked by a poet. Whom to snare first — Celia or Zoe? Although Zoe arrived earlier, I'll let her wait. Waiting has been a strategy that paid off for me. I do, however, sneak a glance as I pass her chalet. She is seated before a laptop near the window. So intent. No wonder she's such a huge success. Whatever was her agent worried about?

After my swim, I nap until awakened by Patrick. He reminds me that I offered to escort Celia into town for grocery shopping. I dislike walking because it reminds me of army route marches, of a wretched time, of wretched sergeants. Walking with Celia and slowing down to accommodate her pace helps me to form a new association with the exercise.

In the Hypermercado, I explained the currency, but she refused to understand. She just handed me a wad of American dollars and said, "Here. You do it."

When we finished, I ordered a cab to *la finca*, and over her protests, paid for it. After carrying her purchases to her chalet, I kissed her forehead and departed.

Upon return to my studio, I was exhausted, but did not give in. I made a pot of tea and set a couple of chops to marinade while I looked over my work, jotting down questions to work into conversations with Zoe and Celia. I dined alone on two superb lamb chops, a green salad and a bottle of ale.

Before retiring, I summon the courage to drop in on Zoe. I have never met her, but her photo on book jackets shows a blonde Mona Lisa. My blonde Mona Lisa. Zoe Anderson. Probably Swedish origin. I open the bottle of Ralph Lauren cologne, a gift from Janine, and dab a bit on my neck. Not bad, really, and quite pleasant for a woman's first impression of me.

When Zoe answers the door, I am not disappointed. Blonde and more Rubenesque than in her last photo, she carries weight well. I turn on the charm, thanking the stars for Norwegian ancestors whose genes gave me hair in which strands of silver make me appear blonder and younger. Zoe is gracious in that "I'm a celebrity, kiss-kiss,"

sort of way I abhor, but I go along with it, surprised that
she possesses what I call "side" and what youngsters these
days call "attitude." She is brusque, determined, I think,
to maintain power. A challenger. She agrees to meet for
an interview "in a day or two." A tad patronizing of her,
after all I'm doing to further her image. Maybe just nervous
and defensive at meeting me? A whiff of her breath made
me certain she'd been tippling. What a waste of Ralph
Lauren! Weirdest of all was that she'd addressed me as
"Derek." After our long correspondence? She was unhinged
and edgy. Overworking, I wager. I was also surprised at
her curiosity about Celia. Good. I know rivalry when I
see it. I'll kindle a competition and start with Celia. Rivalry
is such an aphrodisiac.

On my return from Zoe's, I encounter Mimi, the
child I'd taken to be staff, but a writer from New York.
A youngster I recognized to be a clinger, from whom I
escape on my way to the common room. I'd just e-mailed
Janine when Celia entered the common room. Carpe
Diem, I thought. I not only suggested that she do my
book cover, but asked her to accompany me to San José
for a museum visit. Confused, and trying to create the
impression that I was in Costa Rica with high inten-
tions, I picked up a book about butterflies and a short
story collection. I don't have a clue about butterflies and
loathe short stories.

I've been playing the gallant escort to Celia. Before
our gallery trip, I ordered our taxi and arranged for a
tour of art venues. Ladies do like what they refer to as "a
take charge kind of guy." More bizarre is their awe when
they learn that the guy speaks a foreign language and
knows about food and wine.

In San José, I was pleasantly surprised to find that Celia possesses a broad knowledge of the arts. And by the fact that, eager to please, she had dressed well. I chose the dining room of the Hotel Juan Carlos for its quiet elegance. I'd guessed her type and although craving curry and a beer myself, ordered a Spanish-y luncheon and cheap bubbly, which seemed to delight her. There was the usual North American struggle over the bill, but again, I insisted on paying. Money is power and I intend hold on to it.

Besides, Celia deserves a treat. The poor dear won't be happy very long. For days the e-mails from Toronto and points north have been saying that Mel has dug her hooks in. She's off to Havana with John. This development calls for a change of strategy. Celia will head home when she finds out, which given e-mail, will be soon. I'll provide the supportive shoulder she needs while further inciting rivalry between her and Zoe.

As I shut down the computer, Mimi enters in a tantrum at being dismissed by Celia. I can't abide a woman in tears, so seize Mimi's shoulders and commanded. "Listen to me, young lady!" She not only shuts up, a glimmer of a smile crosses her lips.

Although I doubt her ability to be discreet, her response to my firm stand leads me to trust her and tell her about Celia after swearing her to secrecy. "Girl, get over yourself! Our poor, dear colleague faces a difficult time. She doesn't know yet, but she's about to be rejected by a man she's been faithful to for years. I beg you not to tell anyone until she finds out herself. She'll need all the support we can muster. Get that!"

I felt like one of my old sergeants, but it worked like

a charm. I sensed that she needed a firm hand. I obliged when she requested "another shot," and posed in front of the computer for her. She'd even brought along a copy of my book, *Of Poetics and Feminism*, which required another shot of me while holding it and of course a request to autograph it. Obviously she's a serious writer, unlike the library dolts. The child told me she's studying creative writing in community college but even with her interest in criticism, I feel that perhaps she would be best served by her little camera. She seems adept enough, and God knows she's keen.

After she was through "shooting" she showed great compassion for Celia and asked me to tell her more.

"You mean to say that nice elderly lady has been dumped by a *husband*? What's going to happen to her? Who'll take care of her?"

I was surprised by all this sympathy, if annoyed by her reference to Celia as "elderly." I insisted that she keep the *dumping* of Celia quiet until if and when Celia herself learned the news. I felt that I'd handled the whole thing rather well. I realized that I'd misjudged the young woman. The child needs nurture. In some ways, she reminds me of Janine. Her compassion.

Indeed, Mimi does seem to have more to her than I have thought. Apparently she's made friends with Zoe. As I leave the common room I see her head for Zoe's studio. I return to my studio and bed down for the night. Alone. I'm increasingly irritated by Zoe's avoidance of me, but know that she is working hard. I'll bide my time. On the other hand, she seems to have lots of time for Mimi in the evening. Every night the two of them take off in a taxi. She's probably taking the youngster under her wing.

It's obvious that the child has rough edges and needs guidance but that's no excuse for Zoe to avoid me.

I catch up on e-mails, swim daily, read and go over notes while awaiting Zoe's summons. Celia has stopped coming down to the common room. A day or two ago I glimpsed her in the bushes cutting down branches and toting them off. Not a sight since.

Christmas Day was, as Mimi would say, "a drag." After sharing a drink with Patrick and Margo, I escorted Mimi into town for a proper Christmas dinner. Heavens, that little lady has an appetite! I felt obliged to, because the child has been following me around, yakking about "the Net," asking about poetry and taking my picture. The girl hasn't a clue, but missing Janine, I do the fatherly thing.

In the evening, I go over to the common room and find Celia there. I hesitate when she asks me to telephone John in Havana for her. Dear God, surely she hasn't found out.

I try to avoid this task, but Celia insists. She will doubtless leave early and head home to deal with legalities when she does find out about Melanie. But for now, she needs a strong shoulder. After that, I'll be free to pursue my relationship with Zoe.

Zoe is distant — still playing hard to get, but competition will make her bite when she learns that I've spent the night with Celia.

I'll comfort Celia over that Glenlivet I purchased at Duty Free. A fine malt that's pricey back home. I had plans for that bottle. As A. E. Houseman wrote long ago, "Malt does more than Milton can." Good man. It does indeed.

I retrieve the Scotch, climb up to Celia's studio and wait outside. Having decided to make it a night, I avail myself of one of the prescribed pills. After all Celia has been through, I'd hate to disappoint her. The Ralph Lauren cologne will make our experience all the more memorable for her.

I hold the bottle high and wave.

Celia

Artists love to immerse themselves in chaos in order to put it into form.

Rollo May

I carry my equipment outside, set the oil sticks in a row and kneel on the grass under the blazing sun.

I arrange three stalks of *heliconia*, with those amazing purple-edged orange blossoms, in a jar of water set just inside the door. More sharply colored than bird of paradise blooms, but a similar shape. Gorgeous!

What shades to use? Let me see . . . powerful vermilion in the centers . . . for the furry edges, something bluish. Indigo?

When I hold the oil sticks in my fingers, I feel like a little kid playing with crayons, not a grown-up artist.

I'm enough of an artist to have a Toronto dealer. Above a Sunday painter and below the Group of Seven. Snowbound professionals buy my work, craving tropical colors to lift their spirits and match their sofas and armchairs. Trendy decorators buy them to grace southerners' Sudbury summer retreats. A North Bay politician bought three for his Toronto condo to show his support of local talent. That was back when he was still in office and I still endured Canadian winters.

My dealer wants a show in March. *"Las Flores de Costa Rica."* Crowd pleasers, showy stuff for posters. What doesn't sell in Toronto I'll tote home to Sudbury and sell at The Tundra. It's a living. I'd hoped, as an artist, to be bigger and better, but I learned to settle for less.

I need to soak up sunlight to beat depression. I crave light even if it means being away from John. Or because it means being away from him. My doctor prescribed Xanax, but what does he know?

John's in Havana preparing for Cuba's Book Fair while Melanie Black, a young writer, minds the bookstore. I adore Cuba, but don't even try to work there. Cubans keep dropping in to invite us to parties. In Havana, I just give up and have fun.

John and I accommodate each other. Art colonies satisfy my craving for new landscapes, new colleagues; John courts writers and launches their books at The Tundra. Our arrangement works.

In colonies, artists and writers have affairs that don't count. We go home and it's all over. I was initiated into this ethos at the first colony I attended when I was still a Sunday painter and a board member hit on me. After I'd rebuffed his advances, he told me he'd only accepted me into the colony for an affair, not for my work. I cried a whole day and all night. Raging, I headed for the hills and sketched, sketched, sketched, then went home. I *worked*. Work that landed me a dealer and my first show. That colony launched my career and opened my eyes.

Artists need freedom from convention. For years, colonies met my emotional needs. Now, they're my escape from domesticity and a cold climate.

I got to *La finca de las serpientes* after Erik Bjorseth suggested that I apply. The sunny climate was essential. When November hits Canada, I know why Finns and Swedes kill themselves. So I come south and let sunlight blast me with a seratonin shock to get me through until spring.

If all goes well I'll head back to Sudbury after Christmas, work hard until February, then go down to Toronto and visit my daughter Faye. She's a tiny girl — I mean woman — who counsels abused women. I don't know how she stands hearing their awful tales. No wonder she seemed troubled when I visited her on my way down here.

I work quickly. The noon sun blazes and the heat is unbearable. I'm starving, my back hurts and my fingers are purple, orange and green. I tread carefully and inspect the sheets. Not bad. I gather them up and carry them inside. Work has gone well. I've produced a lot already.

I crave fruit salad and a cup of wonderful Costa Rican coffee. I shower, slide into a new caftan and make myself some coffee.

Sunlight floods my studio. I close the drapes and turn on the ceiling fan. I'm desperate for coffee, sliced fresh papayas and bananas. After lunch I'll pick a few branches of *corteza amarilla* and work inside. Their blazing yellow will be easier to work with indoors. Cooler.

I'd love to swim but now that I'm into my work, if I break, I lose momentum. It's like running a marathon. Not that I've ever run one.

There are two Americans here. From my hilltop chalet I've seen a redhead wander around taking pictures, and that well-known Cleveland artist, Marsha McKay. McKay heads to the river in a taxi and returns every afternoon with a 5x4-foot piece ready for framing. Water colors of naked entwining trees. I envy her speed, stamina and talent. An A+ painter with exhibits all over the world. I'm a B- who has shows in Toronto and Montreal. Her work hangs in galleries, mine in living rooms. The only man here is Erik Bjorseth, who persuaded me to apply. Why? What does he want? Will the usual colony couplings occur? I'd hoped for a fling until he told me he was writing a book about Zoe Anderson. She's here to be interviewed by him. Why here? Why not in Toronto or Thunder Bay?

A knock on my door. It's the redhead. Plump, green eyes, a pale freckled face. Camera.

"Hi," she says. "I'm Mimi O'Rourke. Like, I just had to talk. A few days ago I visited one of the writers but she got mad and said she had to work."

"My dear, so do I," I say, thinking, how like Zoe. Still so very selfish.

"I really need to talk to somebody. I'm upset. Patrick the director was busy, Margo the coordinator was busy. Have you got like a minute? Please!"

I know that Art colony apprehension. Whether one will produce new work or not. I'll listen until she gets her bearings. "Okay, sit down. Tell me about your work."

"My work? Oh, that. Flash fiction. Some people call them postcard stories. I detest that term. Flash describes the jolt of inspiration, you know?"

I don't know. I want to work but am stuck with her. I cross the room and sit down.

She sits beside me, then drops her head in her hands and sobs. "I can't work. My boyfriend ditched me."

"Maybe he worries about what a lovely young woman like you might get up to in an art colony . . ."

"I met him here. Like, last year."

"You stayed together a year? That's a long time for a colony affair. Have you met any other guests yet?"

"Just writers. They're like, *so* into their work, you know? You were nice and let me in."

How to respond? I know "those writers." Zoe Anderson is one of Canada's best novelists; Erik Bjorseth is a South African poet and critic now living in Canada. A charmer. I know Zoe from Vic College in the 60s; Erik, I met recently at a Toronto book launch when I rescued him from a bunch of middle-aged, middle-class groupies. Over coffee, he told me about his life in South Africa and his daughter Janine and Janine's mother, an actress in Capetown; his second wife was one of his publishers' editors. While he drove me out to Faye's in the Beaches he unloaded his story about apartheid and compulsory military service, and we bonded over our hatred of Canadian winters.

The next day he e-mailed me, urging me to apply here and to fly down with him. I'd been flattered until he told me he'd seen my photo in a Vic Annual the same year as Zoe. During the flight he picked my brain about her for his new book. That's why he'd been nice to me. Or he wants a launch at John's bookstore. When I asked about Melanie's writing, he just shrugged. I wondered who had hit on whom, who had been rejected. I'd been miffed after he told me Zoe would be here, but I'd never been to Costa Rica, and had read about the spectacular foliage here. Perfect for my sort of painting.

I'd taken English courses with Zoe at Vic before switching to art college. Everybody was in awe of her. Her brains, her affairs with professors and politicians. She'd infuriated me.

After I left Vic for art college, she sought me out at that all-important first show to ask why I'd quit. When I told her, she laughed. "Because you're tired of words? You prefer colors to adjectives!" She'd made me feel stupid. I was surprised years later, when she attended a show of mine and said, "Now I know how you felt when you left Vic. I'm tired of words, too."

Mimi crosses the room, helps herself to coffee. "I'm from New York. You're Celia Hall. From Canada. You paint. I looked you up. Like, I've got to tell somebody about Jeff. You know?"

"Jeff?"

"My boyfriend? He dumped me. After we'd signed a lease! I'm not only losing him, I'm in debt . . ." Sobbing, she rakes her fingers through her hair.

"My dear, I am sorry. Can't you explain to your landlord?"

"I never had a chance. I just got Jeff's e-mail yesterday." She waves a tattered printout.

"That was cowardly," I say. What I really think is that a colony affair is a colony affair.

Sobs persist. I try again. "Can your parents help?"

"They were killed in an accident when I was little. Grandma raised me. She's in one of those homes for old people, you know?"

She's hurting, but I've got to work . . . Ah, got it! "I have to send an e-mail. Let's go to the common room." A good idea anyway. I've been so engrossed in work that I never e-mailed Faye.

"Okay. I'll show you my fiction. On the Internet. Where fiction should be. Print destroys forests. I'm like, a pioneer, you know? Jeff designed my website. It's awesome."

I lead her away, grateful for crowing roosters and barking dogs that drown her out. In the common room, she darts to the computer, fiddles around and says, "Here's my website, *Mimi's Mini Memoir*. Oh, friends from New York! Just a minute."

"No problem. I'll come back later." She's engrossed. She'll get over Jeff.

I hike back to my studio and pick up fallen oranges and grapefruit along the paths. I hate having to pass Zoe's chalet, but sneaking a glance, see her focused on her laptop. Ever the grind. Same old Zoe, hard at it.

I hear Mimi. And a male voice, an accent. Erik. I look back and smile at the sight of him striding off, Mimi scurrying after him. When I walked to the village with him, I found it hard to keep up with his military gait. Could he be interested in a woman that young? No, she's too naive. A child who takes love affairs seriously. When I saw him at the pool, I thought he'd be a great model for an art life class. Such an amazing body. Mimi didn't miss it, either. There she was, camera in hand. Scrapbook stuff for her to show to pals back home.

After lunch, restless and unable to work, I leaf through *The Tourist's Guide to Costa Rica* and learn about regional flora and fauna. I'm amused, discovering such flowers as *la putina de la noche*, the little night whore; *labios ardientes*, hot lips. Another bloom pretends to be a female bee to lure males to fertilize it. I'll show this to Erik.

Terrified of snakes, I avoid fauna. Locals call the colony *La finca de las serpientes* — the snake ranch. When I queried Patrick, the colony director, about this, he told me that they have killed a few boa constrictors here and then he changed the subject.

I read up on boas and learned that they don't attack humans unless bothered. I keep alert while I walk to avoid bothering any boas on my path.

Enough of flora and fauna. I lie down and wonder about Mimi, Erik and Zoe. Later, I get up and look out at a mountain range — an extension of Canadian ranges I grew up with. Back then I felt they imprisoned me. I had to escape them. Now I want mountains to embrace me.

I stack my dishes in the sink and recall another colony. In Saskatchewan. Did absence of mountains make "prairie people" open and friendly? Of course. Landscape shapes us.

Mimi's landscape — skyscrapers. What flower would she be? Nothing in bloom. A bud.

Zoe, a show-offish bird of paradise. Purple, orange, spiky. Erik, a tall golden corn stalk. Me? A wild field daisy. *He loves me, he loves me not.*

What about Erik and Zoe? Perfect, those names of two tall people. Symmetry. I bet they have an affair. Rumors of Erik's amours abound; and of Zoe's. I fantasize about gorgeous Latin men I see on the street.

It's past noon. The heat is unbearable and I haven't accomplished as much as I'd hoped.

I want a cluster of red-plumed ginger plants. They have nothing to do with ginger. I don't know the proper name so call them ginger flowers like everybody else. I tramp through overgrown paths until I find some and cut off three beauties. In my studio, I arrange them in a jar.

I turn on the ceiling fan. If I close the drapes against the sun I lose light. I'll work fast. My oil sticks will stay firm under the fan.

Working, I lose track of time, try to catch a particular light, a particular angle.

A knock.

It's Mimi. "I have to talk," she says. "That guy Erik was busy."

"Mimi, I can't stop working. I'm sure you understand. Let's meet in the common room later, okay?"

She dawdles off like a kid who doesn't want to go to school, then turns and focuses her camera on my chalet. Handles a camera like a pro, but is really just a kid trying to hold on to a place, an experience.

I lock my door and get back to work.

The sun moves higher, changing the light. I'm far enough along with the ginger spikes to know where I'm going. The heat is unbearable. I put my work in the shade and open the back door before washing my hands and showering again.

Poor Mimi. I'd forgotten how rejection feels. I pour a glass of white wine, carry it to my shaded back balcony and settle into a chaise.

I don't enjoy drinking alone. It would be friendly to invite Erik. He likes to drink but probably isn't crazy about wine. A Scotch drinker, he took hours at the Duty Free, selecting one bottle of the stuff. I'll wait a few days before inviting him. It's too soon. I need to get into my work the first day or I'm lost.

From the balcony, I watch night fall. Up higher in the mountain chalets, first lights go on; down here, bird of paradise spikes pierce shrubs.

I miss John. Habit, ritual. Our pre-dinner drink.

I go inside and make supper. A simple egg salad. Another reason for colony escapes. I've cooked too many meals.

I eat cheerlessly, pour another glass of wine and slouch in the recliner.

What to work on next? What more can I do with flowers? Maybe fruit? Bananas, oranges, pineapples, papayas? Interesting shapes . . . their colors in the same spectrum. I crave yellow.

I'm lonely and it's too early to sleep. I'd enjoy talking

to Erik, but won't barge in. I'll go and watch TV in the common room.

Erik is at the computer. Perfect.

"Sorry," I say, "I didn't mean to disturb you."

"It's okay, Celia, come in. I thought you were that Mimi person. She's a nuisance."

"She's a child. Who thinks her heart is broken. It isn't."

"She's so bloody distressed. Can we help her?"

"We can't. She's young and harmless. More boa constrictor than fer-de-lance. Boas attack in self defense, fer-de-lance kill for sport."

He smiles. "Nice one. You've read the handbook."

"Yes. I do know what you mean about Mimi. After seeing her, I can't get back to work."

"You must, I want you to do my book cover. Wait until I finish here." He returns to the computer.

I wander to the bookshelves, smiling. A cover for his book. Where might that lead? I'm too excited to read, but pick up a Margaret Drabble novel.

"Celia," he says, "how about coming to San José with me tomorrow to do the galleries?"

"I'd love to!"

"I'll order a cab. Nine? We'll make a day of it and have lunch in town."

"You're on."

He takes the phone and in Spanish, orders our taxi. I'd wanted to visit San José, but was edgy about it because I don't speak Spanish. He holds the door and leads me out.

"*Hasta mañana*," he says. He's carrying *Birds of Costa Rica* and *Best American Short Stories of 1989*.

I resist the temptation to ask him up for a nightcap. Tomorrow?

In my chalet, I bathe and wash my hair. I'm glad I had the foresight to bring a silk dress. Simple, elegant and cool. My color. Apricot. I slide into my old tee shirt and go to bed looking forward to a visit in San José galleries. With Erik.

The trip was fun but tiring. Erik couldn't help his stride, though when he saw me lag, he slowed down. He asked me about art and seemed interested in my opinions. It was the best day I've had in years. Lunch in the dining room of the Hotel Juan Carlos, *paella* with a bottle of *Freixenet*. The Art Museum, Pre-Colombian jade jewelry. *Tapas* and *sangria* before returning.

I undress, put on a fresh tee shirt. When I fall into bed, the sheets feel crisp and cool.

Just as I drop off, there's a knock. Probably Mimi, but it might be about a call from John or Faye. I get up to open the door.

"I wish you'd invited me to San José," Mimi whines.

She's not here about San José. She's a child who wants to talk about her little affair.

"My dear," I say. "I must sleep. I'm going back to bed."

She runs off, leaving me too upset to sleep. I have to take a Xanax.

Another knock. Erik? I change into a caftan to answer the door.

Zoe.

"Hi. It's been a long time, Celia."

"Yes." I don't ask why it took so long, or why now. Xanax should kick in soon, so I've no intention of asking her in. She looks well, suntanned. Heavier than I remember, but fit. I wait.

"Celia," she asks. "Tell me all about your trip to San José."

"San José? I loved it. The galleries, the jade museum – "

"Not that. I meant Erik."

"Erik? Oh. Polite as always." Why is she asking me? She's always called the shots. Never gave a damn what I thought.

"Come on, Celia, what's up?"

She's curious. Is she jealous?

"Zoe, he admires you, he admires your work."

"Good. He's why I'm here. The hope of a fling."

There she goes. Competing like she did back English 304. Poetics. I'd led that course until she drove me out of the university.

"Fling away! Erik is dazzled by your work. By the way, he's just been divorced." I wait for a reaction.

"Are you *really* happy, Celia? Doesn't marriage bore you?"

"Mine doesn't. I have a great husband. And a daughter with an interesting career."

She waits to be asked in but I stand my ground.

Finally she moves further out the door and says, "You're tired now. Come by for a chat. Whenever."

"Thanks."

After she's gone, I'm upset. By her visit, her questions. Another Xanax wouldn't hurt. My doctor said it would be okay and for me not to get upset.

It's very bright. I've slept in and missed the early morning light. I rush through breakfast before heading outside.

It's a day for yellow. I'll cut a cluster of those *marvelous cortezas* amarillas. I've never seen such a yellow in nature! Blazing, shining. Past the hedges in a wild spot, I see them and cut three branches, so bright that I have to smile as I carry them to my studio.

What yellow will capture *cortezas amarillas*? Van Gogh's cadmium would come close, a yellow to drive anybody mad. I'll send Zoe my ear.

I arrange branches in a green wine bottle and try different groupings until I find the right one. Elated, I squat on the floor. Even when the sun tells me it's past noon, I can't stop. My yellow fingers fly and smudge, fly and smudge. I haven't felt this way about work in years.

No, I've never felt this way before.

Dammit, I feel great! I stretch and walk to the sink. When I scrub my hands I almost hate to lose that yellow, the one and only yellow that captured the blaze of *corteza amarilla*. I rub Vaseline into my hands, put on the kettle for tea.

I stride to the window and look out at the forest with its mix of deciduous and conifers, at palms that smack my windows in the night breeze. I'm high on a slope of Poas, near the village of San José de la Montana. I'm high all right, higher than I've ever been. An artist's high.

It's this country, Costa Rica. Such light! I've done more than I hoped, caught a flair I thought I'd lost. I'm happy and my happiness is all about work.

I've done nearly enough to satisfy my dealer. I could stay and keep this high or finish at home. It's a tough decision. Very tough. Finally I'm proud of my work and on a roll that could continue. More new work as good as this could take me out of the B- list and up to an A.

I wonder about John.

After the kettle steams, I pour boiling water over the tea and let it steep. When it's ready, I take my cup to the table and sit down.

I sip tea and think. John and I could live here. Faye could fly down to enjoy the sun, get away from those sad women.

Could I persuade John? Should I really leave now when I'm finding a whole new series I could finish here?

I'll go home, leave my work in Sudbury, then head down to join him in Cuba.

Faye will meet me at the airport. Phoning is the best bet. I hurry to the common room where I struggle to decipher the small print on my calling card before I dial.

Faye sounds distraught. "Stay there, Mom. Don't bother Dad when he's busy. You know how he gets. We've just talked, he's okay. It'll be easier to sort stuff out later."

"What stuff? Are you all right, dear?"

"Just busy. Christmas problems. Please, Mom, stay and enjoy the sun."

I'm stunned and hurt, but say, "All right, Faye. I'll do that. My work is going really well."

"I'm glad," she says. "Have a great Christmas. Love you, Mom!"

"Merry Christmas. I love you too, pet."

A bizarre conversation. She's hiding something. About work? A guy? She spoke to John, he might know . . . I'll call and tell him I'm joining him. He hates surprises.

I try the phone, struggling with Cuban operators. Their English and my Spanish are a bad match. Tired and anxious, I'm relieved when Erik arrives at the door.

"Erik, could you help me? I'm trying to call John."

He frowns. "John will be busy. Cubans are preparing for the book fair. Are you sure you want to disturb him?"

"I'm very sure."

He shrugs. "If you say so."

What's up? Why was he discouraging me like that? He dials, gets a Cuban operator, gives John's number, hands me the phone and walks out.

"*Hola*?" A woman's voice. Oh, Melanie. She's not in Sudbury. She's in Cuba.

"Is John there?"

Silence. Is he sick?

Waiting, I hear mumbles. Then John. "Celia, what's wrong?"

"That's why I'm calling you. I've just spoken to Faye. She sounded upset. Is she okay?"

"Faye is fine. Things got hectic here so I dragged Melanie down to help."

Who asked about Melanie? I'm worried about our daughter. "Are you sure about Faye?"

"Yes. We just spoke."

"Okay. I won't worry. You two enjoy yourselves and relax. I'm coming down to give you a hand."

"*No*. Stay there." He pauses and asks, "How's work going? Have you enough done yet to keep Goretz satisfied?

"I'm working better than I ever have before."

"You shouldn't stop when you're on a roll."

"I miss you. Cuba would be fun. I've made up my mind."

"*No*. We've things to discuss when I get back." His voice is strained. "Not now. I have to go."

"Things?" What "things?"

No.

I drop the receiver.

Faye knew. Erik and Zoe — the book crowd — knew. Now that I let myself think about it, I knew.

Melanie.

Melanie and John.

I've got to get back to work, back to my chalet. To work. As I stumble out of the common room, I bump into Mimi.

"Are you okay?" she asks. "Come to my place and talk. I've got wine . . ."

I shake my head and turn away. Then excited, I hurry up to my chalet to work. I'll take as much time as I need to finish more work while I'm on a roll. When I stop to catch my breath, I look up and see Erik holding a bottle of Glenlivet.

He waits outside my door. As I near him, I say, "Erik, that's wonderful! How did you ever know that I'd have something to celebrate? I'm on such a high over my work! It's because of all the light, the colors here! I've decided to stay as long as it takes me to put together the kind of collection I've always dreamed of doing. But I am *sorry*, I must pass on the drink and get to work on a new project. But please, do come in for a minute. I want to show you what I've done so far."

Zoe

All writers are vain, selfish, and lazy, and at the very bottom of their motives, there lies a mystery.

George Orwell

Dammit, here I am stuck in Costa Rica and I miss Thunder Bay already. The snow and skiing, the Christmas lights. In this torrid climate, all I want to do is make love, swim and lie in the sun.

I've avoided art colonies. They're for minor artists who can't afford vacations. Laura made me come here to meet Erik Bjorseth and be interviewed here for his book about my work. Laura demands a new novel. If she weren't such a good agent, I'd fire her. She drives me nuts, always needling me and disapproving of me for living in Thunder Bay and avoiding Toronto. Blathers on about visibility and "the importance of public persona." Lately, she's been pushing me to write, if not a novel, a memoir. What the hell is there to remember?

But it's not as bad here as I'd expected. I really enjoyed the landscape on the drive from the airport — the steep, curving climb up the mountain, clusters of palm trees and little colored houses beside the road. Patrick, the colony director, met me at the airport and had shopped for all my basics. He ordered a huge supply of bottled water. Who the hell does he expect to drink that?

I came ahead of Erik. To recover from the flight and settle in before meeting him. He must have given me quite the build-up, because when I checked out the colony after I arrived, it was obvious that I scored the best studio — the only one at ground level beside the pool. Yeah, in spite of the heat, this colony isn't too shabby.

I set my laptop on the desk right in front of the window. At least I can watch the action. Who goes where with whom. And when.

Dammit, it's hot! Even with those noisy fans going full blast. I take a long shower, and to induce sleep, pour a hefty gin-and-tonic. "Gin and sip it slowly and drink it sitting down." Good old Eliot. I wish I could turn off the bloody quotations. Hell, I'm a writer. What I should turn off is gin — my craving for it started after my last novel when I stopped jogging during the tour. Now, unable to write, I drink. I'd always had to be active; burning energy was my basic need until I hit the wall.

It's been two years since my last book. Will the critics slaughter me? Will whatever I write be as good as what I've already done? What the hell is left to write about?

Laura cracks the whip but I need her. It beats working Publishing Street alone, the way I did when I started. While she hustles in Toronto I enjoy life in Thunder Bay — ski in winter, hike and camp in summer. But I do resent her demand for a memoir. Does she think my muse is dead, or what?

I could write a novel about my university days. That novel would have to include Celia Hall. Both of us competitive. She switched to art college because she couldn't keep up with me. Then she married that philandering bookstore owner. A union that freed *her* to philander and make up for lost time. Pathetic, the way I used men as ego-boosters back then. Celia made up for lost time later, I'm told. Now as always, my body needs men, but my ego is just dandy.

Bjorseth is a looker, judging from his photo. Much as I loathe poetry, I ploughed through his books. Celia will try getting her claws into him. Tough on her. For a change, I want an affair with a guy who's not a jock. Correspondence with a poet and critic will boost my archives for a tax break. "What dire offence from amorous causes springs?" Or vice versa.

How could Celia and I have ever become friends when I had all the advantages? She had to work in the library while all I had to do was study. I admired her, but was furious when she got higher marks than me in some bloody course. Stupid of us both for competing for academic achievement. And stupid of me, envying her waif-from-the-west image — so very appealing to professors. Zoe Anderson seeking power through marks? Men? Dad would laugh. Those were the Birkenstock years. Or did Birkenstocks come later? Yes, we wore Dr Scholl's.

After graduation Celia headed north to Sudbury to teach high school and I went to Paris to write. Dad left me a bundle so I traveled in comfort. Unlike that other trip, the one to England, that first one. Dad was furious with me for giving up the kid. But what the hell could he do for me when he was up in Inuvik? Mom arranged it, so concerned about "our place in the community." The next time I flew it was for pure pleasure; to Paris where I wrote my first novel.

Mom is pleased that I'm a writer because it's something to brag about. My brains are from Dad, a linguistics professor from Minnesota. Weird of him, falling for a provincial like Mom. He'd been passing through on his way north to record Inuit.

If Celia hadn't been so brusque when I went to her show,

I'd have bought a painting. Poor woman, stuck with John Hall. Melanie Black is his latest squeeze.

Why all this late night ruminating? I need another gin. A strong one. I sip it, sitting before my window and watching shadows move outside.

What the hell will I write?

Shit! Here comes some young kid. A redheaded gnome. She knocks. I ignore it.

Knocking persists. I open the door. "I'm working! Don't come here unless I ask you, got that?"

"I'm Mimi. I'm a writer. "

"And I'm *writing* and bloody well needing privacy!" I slam the door.

How the hell did a kid like that get into an art colony? This is not some poor kid's camp! I'm really upset. I need another gin with lots of ice before I can calm down enough to sleep. I'm not used to this heat, that's all.

Ow, my head. Where . . . London? Paris? Goddam sun. *Le soleil.* It's hot! I'll call the concierge.

Where the hell . . . Costa del Sol? Costa something. Costa Rica? Oh yeah. The flight.

I drag myself out of bed and put on a tee shirt and sweat pants. Down the hatch with O. J. Where's the milk and cereal Patrick bought? And coffee? I search cupboards, drawers. Oh, there. Bloody jet lag.

I make coffee and toast for breakfast. At least it's quiet here. Some sort of ranch. They grow coffee, bananas and citrus stuff. I won't go to the village unless I'm out of gin. That I'd classify as an emergency. To appease my gin-soaked gut, I add milk to my coffee for *au lait.* Lukewarm, but a caffeine fix. And it smells great.

I won't write today. It's too hot. I'll just stretch out by the pool and get a tan. I dump my dishes in the sink, put on a bikini, grab a towel and sunglasses and head to the pool.

I lie down on a chaise. This is more like it. The sounds out here are wonderful. Trees swishing, voices speaking Spanish. Maybe I'll learn Spanish. Dad pushed me to learn more languages but Latin, French and Dene were enough for me.

A swishing sound. I sit up and see a dark young man cleaning the pool. So concentrated as he sweeps the water, so serious. He has great legs — the hamstrings and calves of a soccer player. He finishes, nodding to me as he passes. I flash him a smile, but he keeps going.

I wade into the pool. The water is warm. Soupy. Yuch! Give me icy Lake Superior. I swim lengths, then float and think of skiing, of sun gleaming on snow. Cold is in my genes. My dad's Swedish genes.

As I get out of the pool, Patrick's wife Margo arrives with a tray.

"I thought it might be hard at first, getting your own meals. I brought you salad and half a roast chicken. Leave the tray here when you finish. Juan who takes care of the pool will return it."

Juan.

"Wonderful! Thank you. I'll take it to my studio and get back to work."

I carry the tray to my studio, eat most of it and stash the rest in the fridge. I shower and change into fresh sweat pants and shirt.

Memoir. Where to start? From now and work back? From early memories and forward?

To hell with it! I'll play solitaire like Mother did. And for the same reason. Certainty, rules. Something to count on. Red on black, black on red.

A splash. Get a load of that! Erik and Celia have arrived. The guy swims a great crawl. Back and forth, back and forth. Stamina, Nordic genes. He heaves out of the pool. It takes a strong ego and a great body to wear bikini trunks. He's got both.

He strides from the pool and stretches on the chaise. I won't join him. I'm supposed to be writing. Hell, writers are supposed to think, observe. I'll observe Erik and think about Celia while playing solitaire. Red on black, black on red. Where the hell are those aces?

Erik leaves the pool for his chalet. A while later he goes to the common room where Celia joins him. They set off together on a path leading out of the colony. Fast work, Celia.

It's dark. Hungry, I eat more of Margo's chicken and wash it down with G and T. It's good chicken, made with some kind of spicy sauce.

My open laptop waits. A novel is commitment. Not my strength, commitment. I drag out a box of archival stuff and sort through it so that this trip won't be an entire waste.

Later, I watch Erik help Celia out of a taxi. They must have gone shopping. They should at least have asked me whether I needed anything. Margo's chicken won't last forever and I crave my morning croissants.

Another G and T. A strong one. What else is there? I'd have to go to the common room to watch TV so I might as well knock myself out. I'll write tomorrow. I down a gin, make another and sit by the window.

Here comes What's-his-name, my biographer. Erik? Better get rid of him. Mustn't let him know I've been drinking.

I open the door, hold my breath and do the European kiss-kiss thing.

"How thoughtful of you, Derek. The way you've arranged everything for me here. I *am* sorry, but I just can't socialize. I'm hard at work on my novel."

"Splendid! I'd enjoy discussing it with you."

Why is he frowning? What the hell's wrong with him?

"I would enjoy a discussion with you, but not when work is going well. I'll get back to you when I'm free to be interviewed."

"Of course." He waits, looks puzzled and turns to leave. "Right-o. You'll get back to me."

Whoops! Derek? Erik? Whatever. I hope he doesn't know I've been drinking. Being a gentleman he'll put it down to jet lag or something. All I want to do is fall into bed. I leave my desk light on and close the drapes so he'll think I'm working.

After last night's binge, a cold shower will get me going. I need the shock, a relief from the sticky heat. I wrap myself in a terry towel robe that a lover gave me. Tom? Andy? The tall guy. One of the mining engineers.

I slide out of the robe, put on a sweat suit and make a pot of tea. I toast a slice of rye bread and slather it with butter and marmalade.

It was neither Tom nor Andy. James gave me the towel. A cute intern in emerg. The one who set my leg after that skiing accident on Mount McKay.

My laptop waits. As I sit at my desk, I see the pool. Palms cast shadows on water. I could look at that pool all day but Laura will be breathing down my neck. About another novel or a memoir.

As I open my laptop, I see Erik go into the common room. Then Celia. A few minutes later, they stroll out carrying books. What's the hell's up?

There's so much I should know about this place. Who's that morning artist, the one who takes taxis? What's the ratio of female to male guests?

I'll visit Margo, she'll know. She was kind to bring me lunch yesterday.

I stroll over to her office and give her a signed copy of *The Left Bank*, a book I loathe.

"I'm thrilled," she says. "I've read all about you on the Net. Your first novel! Is it sort of biographical like most first books?"

The usual reader response. The usual writer response to that question is, "No it isn't."

Hot to set a record, I say, "Yes, it is."

"Wow! I feel that I know all about you through your writing. I hope you don't mind some advice from a true fan, but I think you work too hard and need a break. I hope you're going to San José tomorrow with Erik and Celia."

Aha!

"No, I'm here to write. I think about work when I swim lengths."

"You're so amazing. If there's anything you need or any way I can help, let me know. I'd be honored."

"Thanks. I'll let you know."

Back in my chalet, all is quiet, all is bright. I'll have the place to myself with Erik and Celia away. Mimi the gnome doesn't count. Neither does the taxi-riding artist. Maybe she has a local lover. Spanish. There's a happy thought.

Not much action out there today. Erik and Celia must be

working to make up for taking off to San José tomorrow.

Dammit, but that pool looks fine! To hell with work. I change into a bathing suit and head out to the soupy pool. I swim lengths until I'm tired then stretch out in the sun.

Sounds. I must have fallen asleep. A beautiful young man leans over me. Oh yes, the pool guy.

"*Cuidad, Señorita*," he says. When I frown, he points at the sky. "*El sol. Esta muy peligroso para usted.*"

Dammit, I wish I knew Spanish. Amo amas amat? High school Latin. I shrug and smile, he shrugs and smiles. He's interested but insecure. I can fix that.

I wander back to my chalet and polish off the last of the chicken, but I'm still starving.

Now what? To bed, or watch for the renegades to return from San José?

Night falls. I wait for Juan to bring back the towel I'd left at the pool.

Erik and Celia appear. What have they been up to? There's one way to find out. It's time to greet my old classmate. As I rise to leave, Mimi darts up to Celia's. What's going on?

She runs back again in short order. Curiouser and curiouser.

I play a game of solitaire, win, then head up to Celia's.

At the door, she smiles. She looks great in an artsy way. Flowery caftan, bare feet, painted toenails. Seeing me, her smile fades.

She holds the door and says, "It's been a long time, Zoe."

"It has. We should catch up. How was San José?"

"I loved it. The art galleries, the museum . . . the food."

"Not that. I meant what's up with you and Erik?

"Friendship. Nothing more."

"Come on Celia, we're in an art colony!"

She glares. "I'm happily married, I'm not interested in affairs. He admires *you*. And your work. By the way, he's just been divorced. Again."

I wait to be asked in. She guards the door.

Poor Celia, so defensive. I say something comforting and leave.

Now what? What about that gnome? Little Orphan Annie. I was rude to the poor kid. I'll make it up to her. I don't feel collegial and I'm sure as hell not maternal but I'm starving. I'll take a cab into the village and take the gnome along. She must know her way around.

I bang on the gnome's door until she answers.

"I'm going to the village for dinner and need somebody to help. Would you like to come? I don't speak Spanish or know my way around. We'll take a cab."

"Like, awesome. I totally know my way around. And I speak Spanish. Just like, high school stuff. Dinner sounds fantastic. There's a little place outside the village, *El Camposino?* Fantastic food. I can order a cab. You mean like, now?"

"Yes."

"Fantastic!"

We're off to phone from the common room before I can like, change my mind. She grabs her camera and asks, "Is it okay if I bring this? I'm like, keeping mementos of my time here."

"No problem."

She calls a cab. "They're like, really fast, the taxis here." Before I retort about people who are like, really limited in their vocabulary, a car arrives. En route, Mimi chats up the driver.

Outside the village, I give Mimi money to pay the driver and follow her into a rustic bistro with dirt floors. We sit down at a rough wooden table. Seeing a bar and bottles, I relax. A waiter rushes over. I'm ready for a steak after nothing but chicken. While Mimi hesitates, I spot a sign on the wall. A poster of a great foaming mug of beer. Yes! I squint as I read aloud, "*Cervezas*." The waiter nods.

"Mimi, you're my guest. Order a steak for me, whatever you like for yourself."

"Wow! Fantastic! That's like, so very kind of you."

She orders ribs and baked potatoes; the waiter is back with our beer and salads. Families smile, couples hold hands. She's right, this is a fantastic place.

"How do you know this restaurant? It's great."

"From last year. With my boyfriend." She pours out a tale of woe about being dumped by a guy she met last year. "This was like, totally our place."

The waiter brings our orders, lifts my empty beer bottle and raises his brows in question. I nod assent and point to Mimi's. I've already finished my salad, but she nibbles hers in small bites. The waiter darts off and returns with more beer, trailed by another carrying steaks and ribs.

She asks if it's okay to take my picture and I nod, ready for a decent meal.

I cut into my steak and take a mouthful. Dammit, it's good. As I wolf it down, Mimi takes a shot of me before she tries cutting the ribs with a knife. She takes small bites.

"For Pete's sake, Mimi, just pick up your ribs in your fingers." As soon as I've spoken, she starts gnawing. The poor kid, trying to act polite or something, when she was hungry.

"Mimi, thanks for bringing me here. The steak is great. Next time, I'll have ribs."

Mid-chomp, she asks, "Do you want some of mine? I've got lots and they're awesome."

"No, just a comment. This is best meal I've had in ages. Let's come back tomorrow."

"Fantastic. Don't you hang out with the other Canadians? Like, have you met them yet?"

"I know them both, but have been too busy to connect. How about you?"

"The guy is like, very polite, right? But that other lady, Celia, is *so* into her work. "

Lady? Honey, if you only knew!

"You were telling me about your boyfriend. Do you think you'll get back together?"

"No. He's, like . . . he's living with somebody else now."

"I'm sorry." I knock back my beer. She takes another photo before finishing her ribs.

"Let's have dessert and coffee. What's good here?"

"Flan. Like, awesome!"

Our waiter hovers, Mimi orders our coffee and desserts in what sounds like pretty good Spanish. That child is full of surprises.

"Where did you learn Spanish?"

"High school and community college. Mostly, I practice with the staff in the home where my gran stays."

"Is your grandmother sick?"

She shakes her head. "No. Not sick. Just like, old."

Thank God dessert and coffee arrive. I was turning into a therapist. And if she doesn't stop saying "like," "totally" and "awesome," I'll kill her.

"It was real kind of you to bring me here," she says. "I hate cooking."

"Me too."

"What about your writing," she asks. "How's it going?"

"Going well. How about you? What do you write? Fiction? Poetry?"

"Flash fiction. They're like, really short stories, right?"

Wrong. Dear God. What next? Nude narratives? "They sound interesting. Would you explain this form to me?"

"I wrote a memoir. Like, on the Net? When we get back I'll show it to you . . . if you really want."

Memoir? At her age? What's to remember?

"Yes, I really want. I'm interested in . . . the Internet."

The waiter brings our bill and I give him my Visa. He returns it with the receipt and I consult Mimi, then add a decent tip. He bows to me, mutters to Mimi.

Outside, Mimi nabs a taxi and says, "*La finca de las serpientes.*"

I'm not keen to read "Mimi's Mini Memoir." Of course it's mini at her age. I'm ready for bed, but after my outburst at Mimi that first night I owe her some collegial courtesy.

I hand her a wad of *colones* for the driver. She pays, returns my change and says. "That was like, really awesome. Thank you."

"You're welcome. Now, let's have a look at your memoirs."

I follow her into the common room. At the computer, she pulls me into the chair beside her.

On the screen, I read MIMI'S MINI MEMOIR. This is fiction? MY DOLLS, MY DAD, MY SCHOOL. What the hell . . . ?

Vignettes. Oh, I get it, These are just really, really tiny vignettes.

AH HA.

I could do that with my archives. Play around with all that stuff I brought.

"I'm really impressed, Mimi, but I'm very tired. I'll see you tomorrow, okay?"

"Totally okay."

I rush back to my studio and go to my desk. This will be a snap. Laura was right. Readers want a tell-all. I can do that.

As I sort through correspondence and old memories, I realize that this will not be easy. I muscle on until I'm too tired to read. It hurts like hell, remembering and reading letters to Mom from England, and Dad's letters to me. Especially reading Stefan's. I ache when I go to bed, but my conscience is so clear that I even pass on a G and T.

In the morning, a fast shower, breakfast and I'm back to work. At first I thought I'd just pull stuff together, but can't stop the memories from surfacing. I write about my daughter, placed in a nice middle-class home in England where I'd been shipped because of Stefan, the putative father and a student of Dad's. I'd wanted to tell Stefan, but he was in Papua New Guinea. I'd waited too long for an abortion so Mom sent me to England. Julia, I'd called the baby. She was born on the cusp of Leo. I like to think of her as a Leo like me. The English nurses wouldn't let me see her, but an Irish nurse sneaked Julia in and let me hold her. I don't even know what her adoptive parents call her. I don't know if she reads, I don't know if she ever wonders about me.

I stop playing solitaire and drinking G and T. I down gallons of bottled water, swim, write, and every night have dinner with Mimi.

After several days' work, I e-mail Laura a draft and receive her reply, "You poor darling, I always knew there was something. It's time to let it go. This is great stuff. More!"

Stuff. Is that all it is to her? Well, sure. Hell, she's an agent. She needs me and I need her. And I need to get on with more of my "great stuff."

I can't be bothered with Erik. Right now, he's in the common room with Celia. No, there she goes up the hill. That awful expression on her face . . . worse than that time I got higher marks than she did. Mimi arrives at the scene, chats with Erik then darts away. At least she provides him with a distraction.

There's no reason for Erik to interview me in Costa Rica. We could work in Thunder Bay, but I owe him for persuading me to come here. If I hadn't, I'd never have read Mimi's memoir and seen how to start my own. She's a cool kid, as kids go, in spite of her weird vocabulary. She and her bloody camera!

I've made plans for dinner tonight. With Juan. He's been sweet, dropping in at night. I'll just have dinner with him and say goodbye. It wouldn't be fair for Mimi to get attached to me. She already has a rotten mother in Florida.

She's at my door, panting. I let her in, but want to get back to work. "Please, hurry, Mimi. What is it?"

"We've got to help poor Celia, right? She's so upset! She just like, found out her husband has been cheating on her."

I'm pissed off by her obvious delight in bearing what to her is sensational news and by her continuing use of "like," "totally" and "awesome."

"I'm sorry, Mimi, neither of us can help her. I knew that this was bound to happen. Now, please leave and let me get back to work."

She stands there looking stricken. Either from concern for Celia or from disappointment that I don't find her revelation as dramatic as she does. I turn away and get back to my laptop.

She dawdles a moment before scooting off. One more dinner with her is all I can take. Totally.

Poor Celia. The last time I saw her she was out in the bush hacking blossoms. More crap floral art to match crappy furniture.

The days have flown. With Laura's blessing, I'm heading home to Thunder Bay to catch some skiing. As soon as the season starts, one of the engineers is going to take me ice fishing.

Tonight at our farewell dinner, Mimi and I both had roast lamb and flan.

I was worried because the girl was starting to cling. She seemed to be obsessed with me and kept taking my picture. When I learned that she was also "shooting" the others, I put it down to a loser basking in the light of famous associates and needing something to show off back at home. Poor kid. I promised to keep in touch with her by e-mail. It's the least I can do.

Mimi

Beginners are subject to trial by market, poor things.

Robert Frost

This year I'll work real hard and make my name as a writer. If nothing new inspires me, I'll just finish that old work-in-progress I sent the colony last year. I tried to arrive ahead of the others to scope stuff out and soak up atmosphere because Mr Parsons told our writing class that sense of place is like, vital. But what the heck does sense of place matter if the characters are *boring*? I thought that the writers and artists coming here could be characters for my work-in-progress so wanted to pick Margo's brain before they got here. Then some darn Canadian novelist I'd never heard of arrived, so there goes that plan.

I'm so doggone tired. It was the pits, having to finish up at work before catching the red eye from New York. Hanging out in Miami while waiting for the plane to Costa Rica was sort of interesting with so many tourists around. All those old people from Canada in their new summer outfits.

After I got in last night I couldn't sleep. Like, hundreds of dogs barking and weird scratchy noises on the window. I really miss street action. Traffic and people talking. I don't miss my dumb job typing reports for the Feds even if it is steady and pays well. Same old, same old. At least it's nice and warm here and there's no snow to remind me of Christmas. If I think of Christmas, I miss Gran. It's been two years since she went into that cruddy seniors home. Before then, she always tried to make holidays special for me. They were special anyway because Mom was away, off in search of new guys.

I might as well visit that Canadian writer to find out what's so special about her. It made me mad the way Patrick like, totally fussed over her when she arrived. Doing her shopping and meeting her at the airport. It's not fair to give some guests special treatment just because they're already famous. Could be there's another reason, like a back story. Maybe somebody she loved died and she's here to get over it and write about it as therapy. After Patrick set her up in the best studio, I watched her wander around and sort of check the place out. She's probably lonely and would welcome a literary chat with another writer. She might take me under her wing and like, make me her protegee. I could use that. Yeah, I'll go and pick her brain while she's all alone and needs company.

I stroll over to her place and knock on the door. I start to introduce myself and she yells at me about being "a writer in need of privacy." Well duh! I was just being nice. She appears to me to be a disturbed woman with major problems. She's a major lush — the smell of booze nearly knocked me over. She's at least forty, but not bad looking for that age.

I head to the common room to read the guest list. "Zoe Anderson, Canadian novelist." Zoe Anderson needs a shrink or membership in A.A. Also, "Erik Bjorseth, critic and poet." Bjorseth? What kind of a name is that? Something foreign. "Celia Hall, Canadian painter." Jeez, don't Canadian artists ever work at home? I've given up on Cleveland painters. Anti-social. But that's Cleveland.

There goes Juan to clean the pool. Last year I was too busy with Jeff to get to know him. I bet he knows a lot about what goes on here.

I yell, "*Hola!*"

He smiles, but when I go to the pool he won't even look at me and keeps on working. I sense something very wrong with this place this year. Totally. Toxic, bad vibes. First, that really sloshed writer. Now Juan won't even talk to me. He'll come around. I know Spanish guys.

Last year was awesome. I was excited, being among other writers, but my creativity never emerged until I met Jeff. This year, even Patrick isn't friendly, and as administrator it's his job to be nice. When I got in last night, he said, "Be a good girl and behave." Like, I wasn't supposed to fall in love last year? Or is he still pissed off because I got in last year after he rejected my application? Somebody dropped out while he was away and the committee accepted me. Margo is a whole other matter. Like most women her age, she's totally threatened by young women. This place needs a resident shrink, my psych course taught me that much.

I was so scared after I first arrived here last year that I felt like giving up and considering another career. But as soon as I met Jeff, my creativity took off. Then he encouraged me to write my memoir, showed me how to put it on the Net and all of a sudden I was a hot young writer out there for everyone to read about! Awesome. After I saw my memoir out on the Net, I realized that print was old-fashioned. I totally love that word "memoir." I dumped the story Mr Parsons advised me to submit, but I'm sure that when he saw my name on the Net he felt rewarded.

Having launched my writing career, I don't feel so

bad about not being able to finish college. I just don't need Mr Parsons anymore.

I wish I could feel like I did last year. In love and writing about it. Writing about one's experience is what art colonies are for. My website advertises the colony, so Patrick owes me. That's probably why I got in again. I almost backed out after Jeff broke up with me. I was so mad at him, I swiped his camera. I wanted his laptop, but the skunk hid it. Without his laptop, I'm stuck with using the common room computer. If I hadn't had a year of psych, I'd call Jeff a heel, but now I perceive that he's just threatened by intimacy. It's a common fear among men his age. At least I'd learned to use his camera and put photos on the Net. It's a real cool camera, a Kodak EASYSHARE. I figure what he paid for it he like, owes me so I didn't actually *steal* it. I'll make the best of things and just have fun with the camera. People love having their picture taken so it's a good way to get know them.

This morning I checked empty chalets and scored some tea bags, a bag of rice and a box of cornflakes. I'll pick up oranges from the ground. It's just so amazing to do that. Much as I miss New York, living in the tropics is an enriching experience.

I go to the common room to send Maria an e-mail for Gran. It's great of Maria to let me keep in touch with Gran like that. Maria is Gran's favorite nurse. I'd feel guilty about being here if Gran thought that I'd abandoned her.

No e-mail from Maria, so Gran's okay. I check the tube-flick the remote and can't find a decent mystery, so might as well leave and hit the sack.

The darn sun woke me up. I forgot to close the drapes. Boring as it is with nobody to talk to, this sure is a nice warm place to spend December. With or without a guy.

This year I'm going to make it. All I need is an angle.

I'm starving and there's no coffee, just yucky tea. I'll eat some cornflakes and hang out in the common room before I check out those two coming from Canada. If Juan's at the pool, I'll go for a swim after I e-mail Maria. It's a nuisance working in the common room. Big mistake to swipe Jeff's camera and not his laptop. But I'll like, remain positive and make the best of things.

I pass that totally disturbed writer at her window. She's at her laptop, working. One of those workaholics I've read about. No wonder she's famous in Canada. Maybe it's the winters up there. Too cold to do anything but work, work, work. I'd never give up on real life like she does.

Wait a minute . . . I grab my camera and shoot. Awesome! "Writer at Work." "Writer as Slave to Booze." Maybe I'm really like, a photographer. Maybe my tool is my camera. Maybe this was like, meant to be.

Mr Parsons insisted that journaling is vital for writers, but nothing worth journaling has happened yet and I don't know how to pass my time. TV? A book? Here's one by that Erik guy. *Of Poetics and Feminism*. Bor-ing. I'll carry it around to show Margo and Patrick that I'm seriously committed to a writing career and deserve to be here.

I hate being alone and feel worse after that writer was so mean to me. I'll walk into the village and grab a taco or something. I like the way the hot dark guys down there stare at me.

On my way, a taxi stops at the colony gates. Bundles of art supplies are strapped on the roof. What a drag, having to carry all that stuff around! The car starts up again and when it passes, I see a big blond guy. Hot. The lady looks sad. I'll hang out in the village until they're settled. Before

I visit, I'll give them a day or two to get used to the climate and everything.

The lady must be that artist, Celia Hall. Maybe she'd like to paint my portrait so I can put it on the Web. I'll find an angle. She looked motherly. Not like Mom, drinking her way through early bird specials down in Florida with whatever dude she picks up this year.

Yeah, after Celia is settled, I'll visit her place. *Studios,* the artists call their places. So snooty.

In the village, I hang out at a taco joint. I flirt with the guys and surprise them by speaking Spanish but I don't lead them on. Because I act shy, they treat me with courtesy.

Walking back makes me hungry again. As I pass the pool, I see a hunk standing on the diving board. Awesome bod. It's that guy in the cab. Erik? This year could be even better than last year. Meant to be, like kismet.

I take my camera and shoot. Maybe Erik will be my mentor and help me with my work-in-progress. He impresses me as being a person of class. When he sees me shooting, he waits a bit before he dives, which gives me time to get a perfect shot. It's like, almost as though he's posing for me.

I check my e-mail again. *Nada.* Guess Gran's okay. I go back to my place and watch the action.

There goes the Erik the hunk all dressed up, heading over to Zoe's. I'll nail him before he gets the brush-off.

Jeez, he's a fast walker. I catch up. "I'm Mimi — "

"Good afternoon. I'd love to talk, my dear, but I have a conference with another writer. Would you excuse me for now? We'll chat later. "

"Of course. I'm a writer too, I totally understand."

What a smile! It's his great teeth. He comes from money.

You can always tell by people's teeth. White and straight means good dental care, and dental care costs money.

I'll wait inside and keep track of how long he stays with Zoe.

Whoops! The door-slamming treatment. Not a good time to nail him. He heads into the common room looking worried. Later, Celia goes in and they wander off somewhere. Probably just going for a walk.

They return in a cab and unload groceries. I wonder if they're a couple? It's hard to tell at colonies. I'll check Celia out tomorrow.

I left those two from Canada alone yesterday. Time to check them out. If Juan's at the pool, I'll swim.

It's quite a hike up to Celia's for someone as old as she is. It's one of the biggest studios. I could trade with her, mine's down where it's easier to walk. I'd do that for her. Gosh, it's nice up here with all the bright flowers and shrubs and stuff.

I knock before I open the door then walk right in. At first, she seems glad to see me, then not so glad. I need to get her interest . . . Sympathy?

She has coffee. I grab a mug and help myself. Get the tears going. This is like, a real neat place to hang out.

Celia acts sort of desperate. Could be she's peri-menopausal. When she doesn't open up, I pump her about the other artists because I want to know all about Erik. He's the kind people talk about, a guy who gets around. I've read about men like that — alpha males who work their way through groups of women. There's one at every colony, someone told me.

"I dropped in to get acquainted, Celia. I'm Mimi O'Rourke.

I just had to talk! I tried to make friends with those other Canadians, but they're so mean! They wouldn't give me the time of day. Patrick and Margo are both busy. Have you got a minute? Please! That writer told me she had to work!"

She frowns. "My dear, so do I."

It's so nice, the way she talks. Calling me, "My dear." Cool. I want to get on with things, and like, observe her body language. I try turning on the tears. "I've got to talk to somebody! I'm so upset." The usual.

She melts and asks me about my work. Well duh! I try to explain about flash fiction but she just isn't getting it. When I do the poor-little-me-after-Jeff-left routine, she bites.

She starts to play Ann Landers. Bor-ing! I let her ramble and make nice, until she starts in on Zoe. Oh. A reaction. She stops to think for a while before she delivers the goods.

"Zoe Anderson is a Canadian novelist. Erik Bjorseth is a poet and critic living in Canada. He's from South Africa."

I just knew there was something foreign about Erik.

Celia is restless. Time for more tears and my Jeff story. "I've got to talk to somebody!"

She sighs, then goes motherly. "Of course. I'll listen."

Blah, blah, blah.

"I've seen you out with a camera. Are you working on a photography project?"

"Not really. It's just a hobby that inspires my writing."

"Interesting," she says.

Pretty soon she tells me she has to work and makes some dumb excuse about sending an e-mail. Well, duh, another one with no time for others. I go with her to the common room because I need to use the computer anyway. I show her my memoir but she just doesn't get it. You'd think an older artist would keep up with new media and young writers.

I check my e-mails. Nothing from Maria. I was worried that Gran might miss me and start acting up. No news is good news. Nothing from Jeff, not that I care. At least the dork left his share of the rent, though it makes a better story telling people he didn't. Maybe it was all for the best. Erik seems to be a better role model for the kind of famous writer I see myself becoming.

There he goes now into the common room. Maybe he's looking me up on the Net. It wouldn't be a good time to nail him. Before I quit watching, Celia goes to the common room and a while later they come out carrying books. Just a couple of grinds.

I take a stab at reading Erik's book but it's too deep. So many words to look up.

I'm hungry. It's time to go back and visit Celia with all that stuff in her fridge. This time, she holds the door and says she wants to work, but she's a sucker for tears. I saw her getting lots of work done outside her place later this morning.

"Celia, I'm still upset and need to talk. That guy Erik was busy."

"Mimi, I've made a productive start. I'm at a trying part of my work and can't stop. You're a writer so I'm sure that you understand."

Blah, blah, blah.

At least she like, respects me as a writer. I just timed it wrong. I leave with a hurt look.

At my place, I eat the rest of the cornflakes and an orange. Still no coffee. Tomorrow I'll have tea and another orange for breakfast. I'll pick more oranges and grapefruit. I'm totally bored, hanging out in the common room to watch TV, so hit the sack early.

What's that sound? I roll out of bed and go to the window. What do you know, it's the old-timers going off in a cab. Probably to San José. They could have been friendly and invited me along. I'll find out what went on from old Celia. She'll be all show-and-tell when she gets back.

I eat an orange and drink a cup of tea. I'm starting to like tea. With that accent, I bet Erik drinks tea.

After breakfast, I try again to read Erik's book, but, duh! Who reads that stuff? Heavy.

I pass the morning taking shots of flowers. Whoops, I hope that time doing this hasn't got me into trouble, here comes Margo.

"Mimi, why didn't you tell us that you were also a photographic artist? I've seen you taking shots of colony landscape. Those could really encourage other artists to apply. You've been too modest."

"It's really more of a hobby. I thought I'd post the good ones on my website."

"You go right ahead and do that!"

She was cooperative about posing and said that nowhere on the colony was out of bounds to me.

All afternoon I Google the other guests. I find lots of cool stuff on all of them. I'm so-o taken with Erik, and judging from what's on the Net, he's seen lots of action. Married twice. I knew it. Typical alpha male.

Time for a break. I'll walk into town and grab a snack. I like the way the dark guys here stare. Hot.

I order a taco in high school Spanish. Another American advantage. The Canadians speak French, no good here. I decide that I'm mad at Celia and Erik for taking off like that without asking me to come.

On my way back, I figure I'll have another try with Juan.

He must get lonely, working so hard. He's cleaning the pool, but that awful Zoe is lying out there. Darn it!

Back in my place, I make an effort to understand Erik's book. It's so boring that I fall asleep.

I wake up when a car passes. From my window I see Erik and Celia getting back from San Jose. Did they shack up? At her age, even if they didn't do anything, Celia will want to talk about it. Brag. She'll get a guilt trip from me. It's really mean of them, leaving me here alone while they take off. If Celia expects a visit from Erik tonight, I'll go right up there and fix that.

Door's locked. I knock louder. Maybe Celia's asleep. Maybe even dead at her age.

When she finally answers the door, she's got on a big T-shirt. She's too old for a T-shirt, but it means she's not expecting company.

"Mimi, I'm very tired and I was already in bed."

Yeah, right.

I pass Zoe on my way down, and just to be polite, say hello, but not like, in a friendly way. Not after the way she snubbed me that first day. I wonder how she'll react when she finds out that Erik the hot guy was in town all day with Celia.

I watch. What's going on up there? They're talking at the door but Celia doesn't ask her in. Like, really rude, but why blame her? Zoe is ruder.

Should I check my e-mails again? Have another go at Erik's book? Eat another darned orange?

Well, look who's heading here. Zoe.

I let her wait. She seems mad about something. I never did anything, why is she bothering me?

I open the door and she's all smiles.

"I want to go into the village for dinner and need someone to help me. Would you like to come? I don't speak Spanish or know my way around. We'll take a cab."

Well, duh! Boy, I'm glad I kept up my Spanish.

I make nice even if it seems weird. She lets me take over and pick the place to eat. I sure hope she's paying. I phone a cab, a driver I know from last year. I sit in front with him.

At El Camposino, she asks me to order steak for her and whatever I want for myself and lets it be known it's all on her. Before I can even order, she reads a sign on the wall with a picture of a bottle and asks the waiter to bring us *cervezas*. It's interesting what people pick up first in a language. I knew it. A lush.

"Would it be okay if I took your picture? I'm making an album, like, pictures of famous people and scenery. For souvenirs. Everything here is so pretty."

She stops downing her beer long enough to say, "Sure, go ahead."

I shoot her draining the mug.

I stay on my best behavior. When she asks me about myself, I tell the sad story about my boyfriend and play dumb, her fan.

She has one huge appetite, the way she put away that steak. It seemed polite to offer some of my ribs, since she's paying. But no, now she wants dessert and coffee. Awesome.

We have a totally close time sharing life stories. Maybe she's over her period or whatever it was that was making her so mean to me before.

While we eat dessert, she asks about my work. She's not up on flash fiction either and doesn't sound too speedy about the Net. I offer to show her my work when we get back. I snap a few shots of her inhaling dessert. Too bad she smeared creme caramel on her face.

She gives me her Visa and lets me handle the bill. After that's settled, I nab a taxi. Seeing how nice she's been, I offer to show her my website and bring her up to date on current technology.

Like, really friendly, she says, "Yes please, I'd love to have a look at those memoirs of yours."

She squints as if she has some sort of eye problem. Or trouble focusing. After a while she seems to focus. She nods as if she likes what she sees, then seems in a hurry to leave. At her age, she needs to hit the sack.

Every night after that, we go to El Camposino. I'm eating awesome meals and having fun with my camera.

I'm miffed with Juan. I'm not a one-night-stand sort of person but he hasn't come around to see me since our first night together. Typical Spanish.

It's a good thing Zoe is suddenly busy every day. I work until dinner time doing research, taking photos and observing. I was going to put my photographs on a blog, but got the idea of querying that tabloid publisher, *Slap Shots*. I sent them some samples of my stuff and got a response right away. I never dreamed that my hobby would make a big hit with a major magazine.

I'm still having a heck of a time with Erik's book and have to look up a lot stuff he writes about. When he took me into town for Christmas dinner, I thought this was the start for us, but he was like, a perfect gentleman. Too much so, if you ask me.

I e-mail *Slap Shots* more of my photographic work. After I finish, I try the tube, hoping to find a good mystery. I can't find anything, so go back to my place.

As I leave, Celia goes in the common room, then Erik. Celia runs out and Erik rushes back to his chalet. The jig's up, that stuff he told me about her husband. I'll wait, then drop in on the old lady and say I'm worried about her. I'll visit Celia first to see if I can help her, then visit Erik. It's time I got a piece of the action.

On my way to comfort Celia with a bottle of wine, I see Erik hiking up to her studio with a bottle of hard stuff. I bide my time and get a shot of him outside Celia's chalet waving the bottle in the air. I get another of him coming back alone still clutching the booze.

It's like a little story in itself. With a plot and everything. Mr Parsons would be proud of me but I realize now that fiction is just not my thing. I'm too outgoing to lock myself up and write all day. Literary hermits, is all writers are. My gift lies in recording the lives of others.

It sure pays better. After I sent the last batch of photos to *Slap Shots*, they offered me a whole lot more than those Canadians get with all their government grants. I never dreamed I'd earn that much at what started out as a hobby. I also never realized that print had so much going for it. I guess I'm more traditional than I thought.

Slap Shots liked that my photography featured Canadians because they're sort of exotic to American readers. The editor had heard of Zoe and Erik and was really crazy about the shot of Zoe scarfing brew and eating with her fingers. I thought my story about Celia being an innocent victim, losing her family and rejecting Erik was a human-interest story, but Celia was mad. She should be grateful about getting a whole new market for her work in the U.S.

I'm following up on another story about a Canadian writer — Melanie somebody — who sleeps around to get published. I got that from Erik. My editor gave me the go-ahead. *Slap Shots* is even paying for my flight to Sudbury. Sudbury! It's somewhere in Canada. Gosh, I'm like, going abroad to work. I guess I'll have to buy a parka for that assignment.

I love that shot of Erik in his bikini. Too bad how things worked out between us. He acted like he was my father, yacking about his precious daughter. Not that I know a whole lot about how fathers act, never having had one around.

I'll really miss Zoe. She's so kindhearted. She took Juan out for dinner at Christmas and totally got a kick out of my photographic success. The photo of her by the pool looking sloshed was a favorite with readers. My editor says my upcoming story about Juan, "A Tourist's Plaything," will go over well in New York.

Best of all is my close friendship with Margo and Pat. Pat says there's no such thing as bad publicity. He's been swamped by applications ever since that issue of *Slap Shots* came out with my first big exposé. Pat and Margo invited me to stay on as long as I like if I need a place to live. I'll return out of friendship and because I like Juan a lot.

Right now, I have personal responsibilities. I have to resign from my job and look for an apartment for myself and get Gran settled into that awesome new facility. The money I've made from stories about this year's guests will pay for everything. I'll have a steady income after I start my new job as a photojournalist for *Slap Shots*.

With my first check for the colony photos, I paid Jeff for the camera. I could afford to buy my own, but like many artistic people, I'm superstitious. I totally believe that this particular camera is my talisman, the way it changed my life.

Besides, I needed closure so that I could move on.